Urban Music Education

URBAN MUSIC EDUCATION

A Practical Guide for Teachers

Kate Fitzpatrick-Harnish

OXFORD
UNIVERSITY PRESS

OXFORD
UNIVERSITY PRESS

Oxford University Press is a department of the University of
Oxford. It furthers the University's objective of excellence in research,
scholarship, and education by publishing worldwide.

Oxford   New York
Auckland   Cape Town   Dar es Salaam   Hong Kong   Karachi
Kuala Lumpur   Madrid   Melbourne   Mexico City   Nairobi
New Delhi   Shanghai   Taipei   Toronto

With offices in
Argentina   Austria   Brazil   Chile   Czech Republic   France   Greece
Guatemala   Hungary   Italy   Japan   Poland   Portugal   Singapore
South Korea   Switzerland   Thailand   Turkey   Ukraine   Vietnam

Oxford is a registered trademark of Oxford University Press
in the UK and certain other countries.

Published in the United States of America by
Oxford University Press
198 Madison Avenue, New York, NY 10016

© Oxford University Press 2015

Library of Congress Cataloging-in-Publication Data
Fitzpatrick-Harnish, Kate.
Urban music education : a practical guide for teachers / Kate Fitzpatrick-Harnish.
pages cm
Includes bibliographical references and index.
ISBN 978–0–19–977856–0 (cloth : alk. paper)—ISBN 978–0–19–977857–7 (pbk. : alk. paper)
1. Music—Instruction and study—United States.   2. Education, Urban—United States.
I. Title.
MT1.F49 2015
780.71'073—dc23
2014035482

9 8 7 6 5 4 3 2 1
Printed in the United States of America
on acid-free paper

This book is dedicated to my precious children. I will always and forever be grateful for the gift of you.

CONTENTS

FOREWORD

A NOTE ABOUT MY MUSIC TEACHER, KATE FITZPATRICK

I graduated from the US Military Academy at West Point in 2007. I am a captain in the United States Army, and I spent two of the past five years in Afghanistan leading soldiers in combat. Fourteen years ago, as a freshman at Northland High School, an urban high school in Columbus, Ohio, I was so shy that I asked permission every single day to sit at the lunch table with fellow students. It is entertaining to look back at how much I changed through the course of high school, but also a reflection of the teacher to whom I attribute so much of my growth, Kate Fitzpatrick.

My band director, Kate Fitzpatrick, was the person who took a chance on me when I could not even figure out how to stay in step until well into the marching season. Kate was also the one who encouraged me (a shy, thin, and not particularly musically inclined female) to play the sousaphone. I was definitely not a logical choice to help fill a void when a large group of tuba playing seniors graduated. However, when I asked if I might try, Ms. Fitzpatrick was enthusiastic. For me, this was a turning point. I didn't know if I could even lift the instrument, let alone march around for extended periods of time. This was the first time I had taken on a real challenge, something I wasn't sure I could complete. I found myself drawn to the uniqueness of the instrument and the feeling of accomplishment when I learned to play and march with it. The next year, I became a squad leader, and by my senior year was elected by my peers as one of the band officers. Each year, my confidence grew and I started looking for more future challenges and unique opportunities, a search that led me to West Point and the military. I am so grateful to have had an instructor who took the time to encourage and help a shy young kid to grow in confidence and leadership.

Throughout my military service, I have sought to emulate the leadership ideals set by Ms. Fitzpatrick. More important than anything else, what mattered most to me as a student was that Kate genuinely cared about me as a person. I feel that the same holds true for soldiers in regard to their leaders. When I arrived to my first unit, 1st Battalion, 506th Infantry Regiment, 101st Airborne Division, I deployed to Afghanistan as a platoon leader less than two months later. My first priority was to get to know my soldiers, to learn about each and their families. Not all of us came home together, some were killed, some injured, but throughout our time, I sought to demonstrate the same poise and attitude shown by Ms. Fitzpatrick.

In the fall of 2011, eight years after high school graduation, I was assigned to be a casualty assistance officer for a mother whose son was killed in Afghanistan. While receiving my in-brief for this assignment, I was called and told that a fellow tuba player from my time at Northland High School had passed away in a motorcycle accident early that morning. At the funeral in Columbus, what was most remarkable to me was how much my classmates and I still looked to her for comfort and guidance, years after we graduated. I think that is a true testament to how much we all love and respect her to this day. Following her example, I sought to offer the same solace and support to the soldier's mother over the following years.

For me, our urban music program at Northland High School wasn't just about learning technical and musical skills. It was a place where I grew into my own, from a shy kid to a young leader. Even though we had few resources, I didn't care at all about what our equipment looked like. In the tuba section, for example, we had names for each sousaphone, such as Big Bertha and Car Crash. "Big Bertha" was the biggest, heaviest, and oldest instrument, while "Car Crash" looked like it had been through just that. When I think about high school band, I don't think about the money we didn't have; I think about the fun memories, the friendships forged, and the lessons learned. I think about how we used to sit in Ms. Fitzpatrick's office or pester her between classes, because we just HAD to talk to her all the time. I think about how I went to her for everything, from college advice to encouragement. I think about my best friends that I became close with as a shy 14-year-old, and how we are still best friends 14 years later. Our urban music program wasn't just an extracurricular activity or a class. It was a place filled with family, and a place to grow up.

I can think of no more qualified individual on the topic of urban music education than Kate Fitzpatrick. In the largest city school in Ohio's diverse capital city of over 800,000 people, mine was just one of many lives she impacted through the high school music program. Kate managed to step into an organization with zero school funding and not only operate but excel. To this day, I maintain that of all my teachers and instructors, both in the Columbus Public Schools and also at West Point, the very best was Kate Fitzpatrick. To those reading this book who are or may be considering becoming music teachers in an urban environment, I encourage you to learn from Kate's experiences and advice, and to incorporate her practices and insights in your programs.

Captain Heather Hernandez, United States Army

PREFACE

I was barely 22 years old when I started my first job as director of instrumental music at an urban high school in Columbus, Ohio.[1] When I first accepted the position in Columbus, I received a lot of unsolicited advice from well-meaning but ignorant people, who told me to "be careful," not to stay late after school, and to protect my privacy. The message that I received from outsiders was that my students would be dangerous, my school unsafe, and my property unsecure if I chose to teach in this school.

---

1. Columbus is the fifteenth largest city in the United States, and Northland High, where I taught, was then the largest high school in the Columbus City Schools, which serves almost 65,000 students.

Other teachers whom I respected told me not to "smile until Christmas," and that I should brush up on my "classroom management techniques." I wasn't sure exactly what kind of experience I was in for.

When I got to Northland, I saw immediately that the population of my new school differed greatly from my own experiences. I was White, and from a predominantly White, suburban, upper-middle-class background. The 1,058 students at Northland at that time were predominantly Black (72.9%), and the proportion of the student body that was designated as being "economically disadvantaged" was over 71% (Ohio Department of Education, 2005). Only two of my students took private lessons, and most of them required the use of a school-owned instrument. When I asked about our music program budget, I was told that we didn't have one, and that every penny we hoped to spend on music, instruments, repairs, and supplies needed to be fundraised. The only thing that I knew for sure was that I had a lot of learning to do.

Then I met my students, and everything changed. We had a bit of a rocky start—they had a hard time trusting me, and in hindsight I know that they saw me as an outsider. It took a long time before we were able to break down the walls between us in order to really and truly see one another for who we were. When we succeeded together was when I decided to let go of the "teacher façade" and "Don't smile until Christmas" mentality and just be myself. I stopped trying to prove myself and instead let myself be as authentic as possible—shortcomings and all. I started to ask more questions than I attempted to answer. I started listening to my students' conversations when they didn't know I could hear them, trying to better understand what their lives were like. I stopped trying to achieve "classroom management" through domination of negative behavior and rather sought to find ways to motivate my students by emphasizing positive elements such as pride and student leadership. It worked. Never in my life have I done something that was so simultaneously exhausting, complicated, joyous, rich, and important.

Having had those experiences as an urban music teacher shapes how I approach this book. I know that I cannot give you a list of simple "tricks" to do in your classroom that will instantly make you a better urban music educator. I know that there is no one but you who can walk your particular path in your particular school to learn the best ways to help your particular students achieve their potential. But I also know that the only way that all of us can work to improve our teaching is to share with one another—our resources, our techniques, our experiences, our successes, and our failures. We walk on this wonderful path to revitalize our teaching together.

Perhaps you have had a similar experience as an urban music educator, having navigated numerous ups and downs as you seek to enrich the lives of your students through music. As an experienced urban music educator, you may be looking to find ways to improve the experiences of your students, and to revitalize your music program. Or perhaps you have never before taught music in an urban school but hope to do so one day. Or you may be studying urban music programs, students, teachers, or schools and want to know more about them. If so, I hope throughout this book to provide you with enough information to challenge those who speak of urban schools and music programs in ignorant, limited, stereotypical ways, and to offer you sufficient resources to make the experiences you have in urban schools successful and rewarding for both you and the students with whom you work.

Although this book centers primarily on the work of urban music teachers, I want to state clearly up front that I believe all good teaching is found in a focus on students. The students with whom I worked at Northland are very precious to me, even though they are all now graduated. I could delve into a thousand stories and still not be able to adequately describe the high esteem in which I hold these remarkable individuals and the extent to which they taught me about life. I echo the thoughts of Janet Mayer, who taught English and Reading for 45 years in the New York City Schools:

> I saw my students as my heroes, who, despite overwhelming obstacles, were not only capable of high achievement but, more important, were also outstanding human beings. . . . They may not be rock stars or basketball icons or movie idols; they are just young people who taught me, every day, how to live, by their examples of extraordinary courage, deep pride, soaring spirits, and unbelievable tenacity. These attributes should count for a lot in life, maybe even everything. (p. 6)

The beginning of any teaching transformation starts with devoting time and energy to learning more about our students and the ways that we can better serve them. Thus, throughout this book I will ask you to focus on the specific needs, experiences, knowledge, and background of your students as the primary resource for designing musical and educational experiences in your classroom.

Throughout this book, I have drawn on my 16 years of experience as an urban music teacher, music teacher educator, and urban music education researcher to provide you with the best information possible. In an attempt to make my recommendations and advice research-based, I have also referenced scholarly resources and studies that have addressed some of the issues that I describe. Some of my discussion is particular to urban settings, while some is just "good teaching" that would likely work in any setting. It is also important to note that my experiences and the experiences of the other teachers that I feature in this book are gained from our work with specific urban contexts that may be similar to or different from yours. Urban schools are remarkably different from one another in terms of their size, the student populations they serve, the resources they are provided, and the learning environment they have developed. Urban schools also change rather frequently, making some of the issues presented as being relevant at the time of this book's publication likely outdated rather quickly. Because of this, some of what I describe in this book may apply to you, and some may not. The best solution I can suggest is for you to borrow from this book whatever ideas you find valuable, draw inspiration for new ideas of your own, and work to find creative ways to tailor these ideas to meet the needs of your students.

With a topic as wonderfully complex as urban music education, you will likely agree with some of the things that I and other teachers in this book say, disagree with others, and struggle to decide how you feel about still more. Deciding how you feel about many of the issues presented in this book will help you to crystallize your own opinions about many important topics that can be of help as you work within urban schools and in urban music programs. This "crystallization" process will likely be of more value to you and your teaching than simply agreeing with everything that you read. Thus, it is important to note that it is your own openness to think about, contextualize, struggle with, agree with, disagree with, and probe for further resources on these issues that will ultimately help you to develop as a music educator in urban schools.

ACKNOWLEDGMENTS

Writing this book fulfills the promise that I made in 2004 to the instrumental music students of Northland High School: that I would carry on their story and their legacy as I worked to do my part to help improve the experiences of students who take part in urban music programs. I am grateful to my Northland students for everything that they taught me about teaching and about life. Each of you has a story that I carry with me to this day, and you continue to inspire me. You will always be "my kids."

This book would not have been possible without the contributions of the five exceptional urban music teachers who volunteered to be interviewed for it. I am profoundly grateful to Deanna Burrows, Victoria Miller, Martha Nelson, Ramon Rivera, and Eric Skalinder for enriching this writing with their stories and advice. I am inspired by the many ways that each of you educate your students through music. I am also grateful to my wonderful editor at Oxford, Norm Hirschy, who approached me with the idea for this book and set everything into motion. You have been a sage advisor throughout this process, and I am grateful for your wisdom and encouragement.

I am profoundly indebted to my extended family for not only their support but also their unconditional love. My family's heritage is rooted in the devotion of amazing people by the name of Eileen and Con Dennehy and Jessie and Stanley Mackiewicz, immigrants to this country whom I honor here because their courage and commitment to their families lies at the heart of my story as a human being. Continuing this story are my wonderful grandparents, Kathleen and Timothy Fitzpatrick, and Mary Jane and Charles Hobbs, parents of 7 children each who provided me tremendous examples of a selfless and hard-working life. I would particularly like to thank my grandmother, Mary Jane Hobbs, for constantly inspiring me with her continuing example of heroic compassion and love. I am also particularly blessed with wonderful siblings and would like to express my profound affection for and appreciation of Ryan and Megan Fitzpatrick, both of whom I look up to and admire deeply. Others in my extended family, related by either blood, marriage, or friendship, whom I wish to thank and honor are Lynne and Del Harnish, my brothers and sisters-in-law, Jack Urich, Ruby Urich, Owen Fitzpatrick, Connor Fitzpatrick, Ronald Frydrychowski, Lucas Frydrychowski, Rylie Bliss, Robert Bliss, my co-teacher and partner in crime Rick Eckler, my first principal Jock Harris, and my student Carolyn Trinter, who is deeply missed. Finally, I wish to express my deep appreciation for my parents, Michael and Cheryl Fitzpatrick, for loving and supporting me unconditionally, always. There are simply no better parents anywhere, and every day I thank God for the blessing of both of you in my life. I love and appreciate you more than you will ever know.

As I reflect upon the journey of writing this book, I realize that I began writing it when I had only one other member of my household and yet finish with three. This would not have been possible without the support of an amazing partner. To my wonderful husband, Dustin Harnish, I love you, I respect you, I admire you, and I appreciate you for your constant, never-wavering support of me and our family. Thanks for being "my rock." To my beautiful children, Carmen Joy and Noelle Elizabeth, thank you for inspiring me constantly to be worthy of your presence in my life. No words exist to express the love that I hold for you, now and always. You are my sunshine! Finally, I give thanks to God for this beautiful, wondrous life.

CHAPTER 1

Urban Music Teaching

A Counternarrative

REJECTING THE HISTORICAL NARRATIVE OF URBAN SCHOOLS: PRESENTING A COUNTERNARRATIVE OF URBAN MUSIC EDUCATION

Historically, urban schools and students have been labeled in stereotypically negative ways. Within the field of music education, this is no different. To get an idea of the historically negative portrayal of American urban music education within our profession, take a look at the following excerpt from the 1970 special issue of the *Music Educators' Journal, 56*(5), titled "Facing the Music in Urban Music Education":

The face of America's cities is pockmarked. Mass exodus has left festering inner cities—domiciles of the destitute victims of disease, hunger, crime, drugs, broken families, and hopelessness. Poverty, segregation, and bankruptcy blight the people and thwart the work of every institution. The poor—be they white, black, Mexican-American, or Puerto Rican—bring their environment with them into the schools. Society's sickness touches every subject in the curriculum, including music. The strain on every subject has been severe. It is breaking the backbone of many city music programs. Experienced music teachers are leaving the profession or fleeing to the safety of the suburbs. The status of music in the cities is crumbling under an avalanche of ferment, frustration, and failure. So serious and so widespread are the problems, that the time has come for music educators to reassess their purposes and their programs. In the ghetto, music teachers find that every ideal they were taught to adhere to seems to be open to attack, or, at the least, seriously questioned. Worst of all, the so-called "tried and true" approaches fail to work. Not a generation gap. But a much more confusing and devastating one—a gap between their middle class values and the particular values held by their students. There is often a vast difference between the teacher's and the student's cultures. The disadvantaged student isn't particularly interested in learning the names of the instruments of the orchestra. He isn't "turned on" by cowboy songs. He won't easily enthuse over studying stringed instruments. He doesn't want our Lincoln Centers. He isn't interested in classical music; in fact, he'll tell you with complete certainty how dull it sounds compared to James Brown or Aretha Franklin. The old image, the old ways, and the old music education curriculum are developing cracks. They don't work in the ghetto. Not only that, there is evidence that what happens on the front lines is becoming an epidemic that is certain to spread to the suburbs and beyond. (pp. 37–38)

This excerpt from that special issue on urban music education was published more than four decades ago, during a time when racial tensions were high and debates on school integration heated. The urban context is referred to as a disease or a sickness. The urban music classroom is the site of a "war" or "battle," and teachers in this context serve on the "front lines." Indeed, the title of another article in this issue is "Teacher Education: Stop Sending Innocents into Battle Unarmed" (p. 103). Urban music students are seen as deficient, defiant, unmotivated, and uninterested. Their families are "broken" and "hopeless." As a field, we no longer see such opaquely racist and stereotypical language featured prominently in our major publications. However, one might say that the negative stereotypes so overtly portrayed in this excerpt still linger today as more subtle, tacit, and, therefore, perhaps, even more insidious assumptions about urban schools, communities, music programs, learners, and teachers. What else can music teachers do than head to "safety" in the suburbs? Who would actually choose to teach "these" students in "this" setting?

Such questions are rooted in a deficit view of urban education (Delpit, 1995; Kutz & Roskelly, 1991; Ladson-Billings, 1994), or a belief that urban students and schools are "less than" rather than "different from" students and schools in other settings. As urban music teachers, we must reject these stereotypical portrayals of our schools, our classrooms, our students, and their families, often told by outsiders who have no real experience teaching in urban schools. On the contrary, for most of us who teach music in urban schools, there is something that just feels "right" about teaching in an urban environment. This does not mean that it is easy. But, we know how smart our students are. We know how capable they are. And we believe they have as much of a right to a great music education as do their peers in other schools.

This book focuses on the development of a counternarrative of urban music education—a perspective on teaching in this setting that focuses on the strengths of our students rather than on their weaknesses. In the chapters that follow, we will explore this counternarrative as basis for revitalizing our teaching. This counternarrative suggests the following about urban music education:

- Every school setting and music program is different. Urban schools are not "less than" schools in any other context any more than they are "more than." All schools, in all contexts, are "different from" one another, and, to be most effective, every music teacher in every setting must develop a contextually specific approach to their pedagogy.
- The "urban" label is helpful only as it helps music teachers identify, share resources, and form community with others who teach and learn in educational contexts similar to ours. Beyond that, neither our students nor our schools can be defined by the simplistic and often stereotypical label of "urban."
- As do students in all school settings, students enrolled in music programs in urban contexts deserve to learn within a comprehensive and adequately resourced music program that provides a deep understanding of, engagement with, and appreciation for music.

- The strengths of our students serve as our most important resource. These strengths become most obvious when we as music teachers make a concerted and purposeful effort to learn about our students: their lives, their abilities, their prior experiences, their existing musical knowledge, their cultural heritage, and their interests.
- As we choose to capitalize on our students' strengths, we must also acknowledge the challenges that many of our students may face. One of the most pressing issues for our students is the existence of a sizeable "opportunity gap," resulting from pervasive and profound structural, societal, and social inequalities often experienced well before many of them first entered school.
- Choosing to recognize our students' strengths requires an openness to culturally specific ways of learning and knowing within our classrooms. Every one of our students is a unique human being with a particular background of experiences and knowledge that affects his or her needs within our classroom, and, as their music teachers, we must strive to tailor the educational experiences that we provide to meet these needs.

By embracing such a positive yet informed view of the context in which we teach, we can reject existing stereotypes of urban music education and focus on serving the needs of our students. Throughout the rest of this book, this perspective on urban music education will be developed in an effort to help you realize your own potential as a music teacher and the potential of the amazing students in your general, choral, or instrumental music program.

Considering Music Education's Role in Urban Schools

The prevailing discourse of the educational environment today suggests that students must pass standardized tests in certain subject matters at ALL COSTS. Schools are penalized, teachers are denied "merit pay," and administrators are fired on the basis of these tests. In urban schools, where students as a whole enter school with unequal opportunities (Lareau, 2011; Milner, 2010), this high-stakes testing culture has caused most of each schools' available resources to be diverted to the fundamental goal of getting students to "fill in bubbles" correctly for a certain number of tested subjects. Although the arts, and music, have always been marginalized in favor of so-called core subjects, the climate has worsened in recent years, especially in our urban schools:

With the arrival of national performance standards and diminishing test scores in urban districts, many misguided educational leaders, far removed from the classroom experience, had the astounding idea that urban students no longer needed a general music class to be an integral part of their public education. After all, many of these students couldn't read on grade level or multiply or divide. How could the district possibly justify keeping a music teacher instead of hiring another basic skills teacher? And so a new chapter in music education was written. The "haves" got more exposure to the arts, and the "have-nots" got less. (Flagg, 2006)

The idea that some students need more math, reading, and science but less art, music, and beauty in their lives than other students do is condescending and demeaning. As music teachers, we must take seriously our responsibilities to educate our students in the art of music as a fundamental part of a comprehensive education to which they are entitled. The life of every one of our students is worthwhile, valuable, and precious, and in our small corner of the world (or our small choir room, band room, orchestra room, or general music classroom), we have an obligation to do whatever we can to nurture our students' social, emotional, and intellectual needs.

Although we cannot ourselves change the educational system, nor can we rectify the profound injustices and inequalities that so many of our students have experienced, we do have at our disposal a subject matter so powerful that many of us would say it has made a substantial difference in our lives and in the beauty that we perceive in the world. Is it possible, in our own very small ways as music teachers, that we can strive to make our urban music program something "spectacular," "wonderful," and "special" in our students' school experience? At the very least, can we try to make our class, our ensemble, or our musical experience one in which every student will find the opportunity to find success in his or her own way? We are no panacea, but we do have something to offer our students that is powerful: the experience of music.

I wish to empower you as a music educator to see the experiences that you provide in your urban music classroom as essential and vital to your students' education, and to provide you with resources to contextualize and invigorate your program so that the learning experiences you provide can be as excellent as your students deserve. To accomplish this, we must for a moment reject the prevailing paradigm in urban schools today that treats music education and the other arts as a "frill" experience at best and at worst a distraction from other more "important" (read: *testable*) subjects. Our urban students deserve to have the opportunity to experience musical moments just as profound as those any other child will know. It is imperative that we find a way to afford our students the same equal opportunities to study, perform, and create beautiful music as those experienced by any other child, regardless of their ability to test well in English or in math. To do otherwise is to doom urban students to a lesser, separate, and unequal form of education due simply to the neighborhood in which they live and thus the school that they attend.

DEFINING "URBAN"

I admit that I find the term "urban" itself problematic, especially if it is used in ways that convey stereotypical assumptions about urban schools and learners: "There is a rich array of excellence, intellect, and talent among the people in urban environments—human capital that make meaningful contributions to the very fabric of the human condition in the United States and abroad . . . yet [many] seem to classify [a] school as urban because of the perceived shortcomings of students and parents in the school" (Milner, 2012, p. 558). However, the term is still frequently used and, as such, deserves some clarification. Despite the negative connotations and stereotypes often associated with the term, many educators embrace the word "urban" as a way to describe their teaching setting, identify with others who teach in similar settings, and seek resources that may be helpful for their particular situation.

Whenever I give a presentation on the topic of urban music education or attend a talk by someone else, I am amazed by the number of teachers who attend. Many of these urban music educators have told me that they often feel isolated in our profession, finding that so many of the resources and professional development experiences available to music teachers do not address their particular needs and the needs of their students. At the same time, I get a lot of questions from such teachers about the term "urban" itself. Teachers in small school districts who are dealing with issues such as high rates of student mobility and large populations of English language learners want to know if it is "OK" to call themselves "urban" teachers. Teachers in large city districts who teach in "lottery" rather than "neighborhood" schools wonder the same thing, as do teachers whose schools are located in the city but as independent charter schools rather than as a part of a large city school district. Next, I attempt to clarify the meaning of this confusing and loaded term.

What, exactly, does "urban" mean? Because the term can mean so many things to so many different people, and because it comprises a complex system of social, cultural, organizational, and socioeconomic issues, finding consensus on a useful definition for it has been difficult. First, we can look at the federal government's criteria for what makes a place "urban." The US Bureau of Census[1] delineates urban areas as those that are "densely developed territory, and encompass residential, commercial, and other nonresidential urban land uses. The boundaries of this 'urban footprint' have been defined using measures based primarily on population counts and residential population density" (p. 1). In general, according to the US government, urban areas are required to have at least 1,000 persons per square mile.[2] Any geographic areas having fewer people are designated "rural"; there is no official "suburban" designation according to the Census Bureau.

This official definition, based primarily on population size and density, is not especially helpful in capturing the complexities of human life that the word "urban" may represent for educators. Indeed, what we typically call "urban schools" can be quite different from one another. Urban, when

1. National Archives and Records Administration (2011, August 24), *Federal Register,* 76(164), (53038), Department of Commerce, Census Bureau, Urban Area Criteria for the 2010 Census.
2. Some areas that have a mix of residential and nonresidential with 500 persons per square mile can also be designated as urban.

used to describe schools, generally encompasses two different characteristics of a school: the metropolitan location of the school itself and the sociocultural characteristics of the students and the surrounding community. Historically, definitions of "urban schools" have also included references to the large size and bureaucracy of the school district. However, with the recent increase in the number of self-governing charter and private schools in urban areas, this is no longer a defining characteristic of urban schools. Large public school districts with centralized bureaucracies still exist in urban areas, but there are now many other urban schools with different school management structures in place.

Milner's Evolving Typology of Urban Education

One researcher offers a potentially useful conceptual frame for how we talk about and define urban education. Milner uses the terms "urban intensive," "urban emergent," and "urban characteristic" to help describe the wide variety of schools which may be labeled as "urban." He describes these categories as follows:

> Urban Intensive might be used to describe school contexts that are concentrated in large, metropolitan cities across the United States, such as New York, Chicago, Los Angeles, and Atlanta. What sets these cities apart from other cities is their size, the density of them. These environments would be considered intensive because of their sheer numbers of people in the city and consequently the schools. In these cities, the infrastructure and large numbers of people can make it difficult to provide necessary and adequate resources to the large numbers of people who need them. . . . Urban intensive environments would be those with 1 million people or more in the city.
>
> Urban Emergent might be used to describe schools which are typically located in large cities but not as large as the major cities identified in the urban intensive category. These cities typically have fewer than one million people in them but are relatively large spaces nonetheless. Although they do not experience the magnitude of the challenges that the urban intensive cities face, they do encounter some of the same scarcity of resource problems. . . . Examples of such cities are Nashville, Tennessee; Austin, Texas; Columbus, Ohio; and Charlotte, North Carolina.
>
> Urban Characteristic could be used to describe schools that are not located in big or midsized cities but may be starting to experience some of the challenges that are sometimes associated with urban school contexts in larger areas that were described in the urban intensive and the urban emergent categories. An

example of challenges that schools in the urban characteristic category [experience] is an increase of English language learners to a community. These schools might be located in rural or even suburban districts. (Milner, 2012, 559–560)

I believe that Milner's definition is helpful, as it recognizes intersections between metropolitan status (and associated issues with the provision of resources) and social characteristics, and acknowledges that not all schools that identify as being "urban" are located within large cities. Later in this chapter, I will introduce you to five highly successful urban music educators. While I spent my high school teaching career in an "urban emergent" environment (Columbus, Ohio), four of the five teachers whom you will read about in this book currently teach in "urban intensive" environments (1 in New York, 1 in Chicago, and 2 in Detroit). One, Ramon, teaches in a school that is located in a "rural" area with a large agricultural base but serves many students who speak a language other than English; who are from populations that have been historically marginalized; are from low-income, dual earner homes; and who attend a school that provides few resources. Milner would categorize this an "urban characteristic" school.

Even as we adopt Milner's typology for explaining different types of "urban schools," it is important to remember that there are both advantages and disadvantages to labels such as "urban." An advantage of adopting a definition is that we can use it to communicate with others in meaningful ways about the context in which we teach. By communicating, we can begin to form networks and communities of others who share commonalities with us. Together, we can share, learn, and grow in ways that would be much more difficult without labels like "urban" to describe our teaching context.

However, as discussed previously, labeling can also be problematic. A disadvantage of using such a term is that it is loaded with stereotypical meanings that may not apply to our schools, our students, or our classrooms. When we use the term, others may assume that this tells them something about our wonderfully individualized, diverse students who are in fact much more complex and unique than this label suggests. The label of "urban" may also be used to exclude others if it is thought to imply some sort of "urban hierarchy." For example, in Milner's typology, "urban characteristic" schools are not "less" urban than "urban intensive" schools; this label is assigned simply to describe a different context in which teachers may teach. We must honor the fact that every teacher, in every school, must learn thoroughly the particular characteristics and makeup of his or her school and students to make instruction more meaningful.

I offer Milner's definition as a way to broaden the concept of what "urban" might represent and to clarify how I am using this term so that you may better understand my particular perspective on urban music education. However, for those who may themselves be uncomfortable with the term "urban" as it relates to their school, I also offer the descriptors "under-resourced" or "under-served," which are used frequently today to describe schools where teachers and administrators must work hard to minimize the "opportunity gap" (more on this later) that exists for many of their students. I recommend that you choose the terms that are most helpful to you in your quest to communicate and network with others in meaningful ways.

We all have a fundamental need to be understood, and part of that need leads us to want to be surrounded by others who share an understanding of what our professional lives are like. Regardless of the labels we use to describe ourselves as urban music educators, we must recognize that our goal is to build community rather than to be exclusionary. Whether we are a band director in a small but densely populated city, a general music teacher at a charter school just outside the city boundary, a choir director in a large city who teaches at a selective magnet school for the arts, or a teacher in any number of other schools that might use the term "urban," we must recognize that we are all a part of the same community. By compiling our resources, sharing our stories, and honoring the uniqueness of our schools and students, we can help to support one another.

SHARING OUR STORIES: MEET RAMON, MARTHA, DEANNA, ERIC, AND VICTORIA

As urban music educators, we don't often have the opportunity to sit in each others' classrooms, learning from each other and sharing ideas. It is also rare that we have the opportunity to attend professional development workshops that are geared toward music teachers, so that we can ask music-specific questions or learn about the ways that other teachers approach similar situations. This is regrettable: Our subject matter is very specific, and our approach to teaching can differ in many ways from that of the other teachers in our schools. We need to have the opportunity to learn from one another and gather ideas that are specific to music teaching, and even more specific to urban music teaching.

To help provide a glimpse into the experiences of other urban music teachers and to provide you with practical advice from those who have achieved some measure of success within their classrooms, I close this introductory chapter by introducing to you five wonderful urban music educators who agreed to be interviewed for this book. Throughout the remaining chapters, you will see quotes from them embedded within the text as well as in sidebars on important topics. They were all recommended to me by people I trust as outstanding urban music educators who have demonstrated the ability to successfully connect with their students while maintaining high musical standards within an excellent urban music program. Although I have tremendous evidence from others that each of them is an outstanding educator, I believe that you will find them not only humble but also ready to share the challenges and disappointments that all teachers face. They are outstanding, but they are also human. Their stories, tips, advice, and experiences are provided not to imply that each has found the only way to be a successful urban music educator but instead to give you support, encouragement, and ideas.

Each of them represents a different specialty within urban music teaching: Victoria is a high school band director in Detroit with 41 years of teaching experience. Martha has been an elementary general music specialist in New York City for 12 years. Ramon has been teaching mariachi for 13 years in California and Washington. Eric is a high school choir director in Chicago with 11 years of experience, and Deanna is a middle school string teacher who has taught for 25 years in Detroit. Collectively, they represent 102 years of experience teaching students in varied urban or under-resourced settings. I asked each of these teachers to provide a "short story" of their teaching career. They have each chosen to share different aspects of their story as they introduce themselves to you in their own words.

Ramon Rivera

Ramon Rivera teaches Mariachi at Wenatchee High School and Pioneer Middle School. In Wenatchee, Washington. He has 13 years of teaching experience, including 9 years at Wenatchee and the previous 4 at Oxnard High School in Oxnard, California. Ramon's primary instrument is the trumpet. He identifies himself as Latino/Hispanic and of Salvadorian heritage, and attended suburban schools himself. The students Ramon teaches are primarily Latino of Mexican heritage, with a smaller proportion of Salvadorian heritage. His school is one that is not easily classified as urban according to traditional definitions. Although it is located in a primarily agricultural setting, Ramon's school shares many of the characteristics of urban music teaching settings provided earlier in this chapter. Ramon is a recipient of numerous teaching awards, including the

2003 El Concillo Del Condado de Ventura Latino Leadership Award for Cultural Arts; the Mexican American Political Forum of Ventura County Diego de Barboza Musical Excellence Award; the 2009 Torch-Bearer World Harmony Award and Human & Civil Rights Award from the Washington Education Association; the 2007 Numerica School Champion Award; the Outstanding Educator of the Year Award from the Fiesta Mexicanas of Wenatchee; and his mariachi program has been awarded the 2012 Washington State Golden Apple Award by KCTS 9 Seattle.

When I started volunteering at the Boys and Girls Club in Oxnard, California, I learned the different instruments and played in the school band. Then, somebody invited me to be in a local mariachi, and I started loving that music and volunteering in the mariachi program. That's when I found my love for teaching. I got to start my first job at Oxnard High School, teaching different mariachi classes. I found it to be a great way of connecting kids to school, providing a positive outlet, and showing the power of music. Students were able to be in the music program and also be successful in their schooling. So, I think it was a great connection there.

I taught in California for about four years, and then I came to Wenatchee, Washington, and I've been here for about nine years as director of the mariachi program. We have over 300 students in the program districtwide, with 14 different classes at three middle schools and three different classes at the high school. We also have an advanced performing group that performs all over the state and represents our city.

In the programs that I teach, the dropout rate has gone down for our Latino students, and I believe it is because they have found a connection to school. They feel a lot of cultural pride, self-esteem, school pride, and that sense of family and teamwork and hard work that our program brings to our community and to their home lives. Where we teach mariachi, at Wenatchee High School, most of our students are from migrant families that work in the fields right now. Wenatchee is known for their apples—we are known as the apple capital of the world—but we also grow cherries, pears, and apricots, and many of our students work in the fields during the summer to help support their families.

For a lot of our students, it's like a family, our class. Everyone knows everybody. Everyone knows each others' families, and I get a lot of the students in class for about six years, and you build that relationship. They sometimes have 10 people living in a one-bedroom apartment, and their families are working really hard, sometimes taking two or three jobs to support their children. Now, they're living in the United States of America, where they can have a great opportunity by going to college. As their teachers, we know what the student is going to need post–high school, so what we do is we encourage them in our music program by traveling to universities, traveling to different schools, and traveling all over Washington to give them that different kind of an experience and to get them to see that education is the key to getting out of poverty. When you work in education, you see that. I think this is a great way to connect: through the power of music.

Martha Nelson

Martha Nelson teaches general music at PS63 in Ozone Park, Queens, in the New York City Schools. She has 12 years of teaching experience, having taught for 1 year in the Chicago Public Schools before coming to Queens. She was a vocal major in college and identifies as White, while her students represent many different races and ethnicities, including many who identify as Dominican, Puerto Rican, Guyanese, Indian, Pakistani, Middle Eastern, African American, and White. She calls Queens "one of the most ethnically diverse places anywhere." Martha grew up in a very small town, where she attended the public schools.

I've been drawn to music all my life, as I'm sure most people who are in this job have been. Everybody in my family is a teacher. When I was a little kid, I wanted to be a teacher, but that soon went away, around puberty probably. And I then wanted to be a singer. I ended up working in the music business for a number of years. I've done pretty much every job in music you could possibly do, from being the performer to working for record companies to working in record stores—all of it. At the end of all that, I ended up without a job. The record business kind of took a nosedive, and I was out of work. In a strange course of events, I ended up being a library teacher on the South side of Chicago in a very, very difficult school that was much more homogenous than the school I'm in now. It was about 99 percent Hispanic, and all of the students came from very poor socioeconomic backgrounds, very unlike my own small town Midwest upbringing.

It was a huge culture shock for me to go into that school, and I was kind of thrown into it with no preparation. I was working as a sub and had no kind of teacher education other than the fact that I came from a family of teachers. I had a master's in business and a minor in music, and I had no tools to walk into that classroom with: I was not certified at that point in time. That was in the days when principals could "squeak things by."

I ended up there, and that was a really a big awakening in many ways. I learned that kids are kids no matter what their background. I was working with first grade kids, and when I asked things like, "Why are you falling asleep in your book?" I would get answers like "Oh, it's because there was a car fire last night in my neighborhood." It was just—for me who grew up in a tiny little Midwestern town, it was a huge awakening.

I was on my way to get certified as a librarian, and life events happened on a personal side that caused me to want to move to either New York or [Los Angeles]. I looked into teaching fellowship programs, and I ended up as a New York teaching fellow. In that two-year program, to be certified, you do a crash course of summer student teaching while you're taking classes, and then you go immediately into the classroom in the fall. I had intended to become an elementary school teacher rather than a music teacher, but my paperwork said I was qualified to be a music teacher because of my undergraduate degree, so, once again, I was kind of thrown in.

I got the job as a general music teacher here at PS63, and started my career over again. This time, however, I had support. This time I had mentors and other things to guide me through, and I was in a good school. I got lucky and landed in a school that believed in the arts, and I got a lot of support that way too. Unfortunately, I had no classroom. I was a traveling music teacher for the first several years here—actually, this coming year is the first year I'll have my own classroom. It is a very large school, with 1,500 kids from kindergarten to fifth grade. There was really nothing to the music department when I came. The previous music teacher was a classroom teacher who played the guitar. When I came in, we started band, a choir, violin, and guitar classes in addition to the general music classes. We've had percussion groups and recorder groups and choral groups, and this year we are even starting a rock band. It's a really rich, rich program now that we've been building it for these past 11 years. I'm so very, very proud of what we've built here.

Deanna Burrows

Deanna Burrows teaches strings at Spain Middle School in the Detroit Public Schools. She has 25 years of teaching experience in Detroit and Boston, including 12 years at Spain, where she also teaches general music classes. Spain Middle School is a hybrid neighborhood school/school of choice, as it draws from the local community but also draws students from all over the district for its performing arts program. She is a violin player and identifies herself as a White teacher of primarily African American students. She is a graduate of the Detroit Public Schools. At the time of this interview, Deanna had just accepted a new teaching position as the orchestra teacher at Cass Technical High School in Detroit, which is the high school from which she graduated.

My story of becoming a teacher includes my path as both a musician and a teacher, because it really was a transformative process. When I was four years old, I went to see the *Nutcracker* with my grandmother at Ford Auditorium in Detroit. I spent the whole time looking in the pit. I don't even think I knew what the instrument (the violin) was called, but I said, let's get down there before he puts it away! So, after I bugged her for years, my mother got me private violin lessons at the Detroit community music school. It was a really excellent, pseudo-Suzuki program. That was the start to my life as a musician.

I started on my path to teaching when I was getting my undergrad degree in Boston in performance. I auditioned at Boston Conservatory, got in, and moved to Boston. I got to teach in my freshman year there, as the Boston Public Schools were "pink slipping" a lot of certified teachers, and they were pulling in a lot of Conservatory students to do some teaching. And so I did that, and I absolutely loved it. At that time, my idea was that I was going to be an orchestral musician, and I was going to these gigs, but the energy that surrounded me in the professional world was just terrible. For example, at break time during rehearsals, everyone got up and packed up, and the excitement about playing music wasn't there. But it sure was in those class-rooms in Boston. That's where the excitement was. I decided that this was what I wanted to do, so I came back to Michigan and applied at UofM, and got my master's with certification so that I could teach.

After I got certified, I got a job right away at Carleton Elementary School in Detroit teaching fourth and fifth grade, primarily. I've been in Detroit ever since. At Carlton, I started a second grade recorder class, which is how I did recruiting. I also had fourth and fifth grade strings, and we did a lot of great things. That beginning class is so magical for me. It really is. And then I got this great opportunity—the woman who was teaching strings at Spain Middle School at that time was leaving. They had just built this beautiful new facility at Spain, and I was teaching in a projection booth that was, like, 15 feet by 10 feet. So I decided to move on to teach at Spain, and I've had a great time here for the past 12 years.

At Spain, I have a fourth grade beginning violin class that every child in the school takes. I started that when I came to the middle school. I gathered enough smaller sized instruments, and, with the way the scheduling was, I convinced the administration that it would be a convenient thing for me to take each class of fourth graders for a 9-week period to learn the violin. Some years I've had a semester with them, and sometimes just 9 weeks.

We would get through quite a lot of stuff within a 9-week period of time. And then, if they really loved it, they could choose to play again in the fifth grade, so that was kind of a recruiting thing too. The classes that I now teach at Spain include that fourth grade beginning violin class, first and second grade general music, fifth and sixth grade beginning orchestra, seventh and eighth grade junior orchestra, and seventh and eighth grade advanced orchestra. This past year, I also taught seventh grade social studies, so I had seven classes with 207 students. Looking back at my career, and reflecting now because I'm about to make this big change to high school, I think that every year that I have spent at Spain has been a high point to me.

Eric Skalinder

Eric Skalinder teaches choir at Thomas Kelly High School in the Chicago Public Schools. He has 11 years of teaching experience, all of which have been at Kelly. He was a vocal major in college (countertenor) and identifies himself as Caucasian, having attended a suburban school himself in a northern suburb of Chicago. His students are primarily Hispanic and primarily Mexican, although a small percentage are of Chinese heritage. Eric holds National Board Certification from the National Board of Professional Teaching Standards. He's also been a nominee for the Golden Apple award.

I had difficulty starting my urban music education career—it was a second career for me. I did a master's program that included teacher certification and then started looking for a job. I figured that with 10 years of full-time performance experience under my belt and a master's degree from Northwestern, I would be able to find a job, and I couldn't. It took me two years, and the way I finally found the job that I have now was through an acquaintance I met whose father was a principal. In Chicago, it was all about who you know.

Getting started teaching choir at my school was really tough for me. I struggled for three or four years, just as sort of a cog in the wheel of an otherwise dysfunctional department and program. I really struggled to advocate for what my students needed. My students were not getting what they needed in the program as a whole, and I felt very strongly that they deserved better. They deserved more from their teachers, from their administration, and from the school in general. So that was a really long, drawn-out fight. And, in year five, those changes started to happen, and the program was given the support that we needed to begin to develop. We finally got some support from our administration for scheduling, programming, and recruiting students. That gave us the opportunity to be successful, when it felt like it had been previously sabotaged in many different ways. Once we got some of that negativity out of the way, it gave our students much more of what they needed to succeed.

The initial challenge was that nobody wanted to be in chorus. I think there were 30 kids out of the entire high school in our elective chorus classes, and there are three and a half thousand students in the school. So, I just went and recruited like crazy. I was harassing every kid who walked down the hallway with a little swagger and talked loudly, who showed any kind of confidence and comfortableness with themselves and their body and their voice, trying to hand them my flyer. The following year, I ended up with 120 students in each of our elective classes, so we had over 200 students total. Once the administration saw that the students were interested in choir and that it was something that was appealing to them, we got more support. The students did a great job advocating for themselves as well.

With those numbers, the issue was that it wasn't a very good choir. They were learning lots, but they were totally inexperienced. Our students all walk in the door having never taken a music class in their lives. We never get students that have had music in grades K through eight. It just doesn't happen. By working to develop the skills of the singers over a number of years, the choir has gotten better every year, because I was able to retain students, which wasn't possible before. Building the skills of the choir over a number of years eventually resulted in going to the city and state choir contests and things like that. And we finally, three years later, received a superior rating for the first time ever.

I am usually given a lot of credit for that, but a huge part is the administrative support and also the support from local arts organizations. An ensemble called Music of the Baroque, a professional chorus and orchestra in Chicago, gave voice lessons to many of our students. That partnership was invaluable; they provided a really top-notch, professional level accompanist for performances and vocal coaching with our students. We also work with another professional group in Chicago called the Lakeside Singers. Bringing in those outside resources was huge for the development of the choir and building the program into the success that we have now. So, we're very fortunate to have that support.

That kind of leads up to where we are now, where chorus has become a cool thing to do in our school, and our community supports us as well. A huge part of what we do is outreach to the community and local churches and funeral homes. Wherever they might need choral music, we are there. We feel like we've sort of established ourselves as one of the foundational components of our school. That's where we are now, and we feel very fortunate to be there.

Victoria Miller

Victoria Miller teaches band at Martin Luther King, Junior Senior High School in the Detroit Public Schools. She has 41 years of teaching experience, all of which has been in the Detroit Public Schools, at both Spain Middle School and King. Her primary instrument is the flute, and she identifies as an African American teacher of African American students. She is herself a graduate of the Detroit Public Schools, and has received numerous teaching awards, including the Mr. Holland's Opus award from the Mr. Holland's Opus Foundation and being named one of the 10 "Teachers of the Year" for the Detroit Public Schools.

Back when I was going to high school, I wanted to be a gym teacher. I majored in music at my high school, Cass Tech, because it was a magnet school for the performing arts, and you couldn't major in gym. My goal was to be in the Olympics, because I could run. I could play basketball and volleyball very well, but I had to cut it out my first three years of high school because the academics were so hard and I did not want to get kicked out of my magnet school and have to go to my neighborhood school instead. So, I had to let the sports go until my senior year. When I got to the 12th grade, I only had four classes, so I joined the basketball team. I made varsity—first string—but when I went to the doctor, he said, you have a heart murmur. You cannot play sports any longer. Now, it would have been a little stupid for me to be a gym teacher when I couldn't play sports. So I didn't pursue that. I became a music teacher instead.

When I first started out at my school, the students hadn't previously had much music teaching, and the school was in a very bad, low-income area. They were all beginners, and I had to start out teaching them the basic things and setting expectations. As I went along in my career, I found that it was most important to be positive and do positive things with the students. My first 10 years, I was doing mostly concert band. I tried to introduce marching with concert equipment, and we did some. Our first parade, I told my students that we had to make sure we marched and sounded good because that's all that was important. We didn't have uniforms. We won first place, and when we got back to the school, the parents were like, oh, we've got to get uniforms. They were just so proud. We had a trophy that was six feet tall almost, and it was just lots of pride.

Eventually I started to travel with my band, and our first trip was to Toronto for a music festival. We ended up with a superior rating, and we had a higher rating than any group at the festival. And so they invited us to go to London, England. So, sure enough, that next year we went to London, and then the next year we went to Switzerland and Hawaii, then Japan. Then, we took a little break because the students got to the point where they felt they didn't have to fundraise as much because people were giving donations. We would get out and sell M&M's and water and different things to make our money, and then people would donate to us. The news media would always come out to support us. One of the men at the newspapers told me the reason they would support me all the time is because my students were out there working, and they don't mind helping people that work and try and earn their money instead of people who always just beg and say, "please give us this." A couple years after that we went to Africa, and I continued to do a lot of fundraising.

I never liked marching bands, but I discovered that the children love marching. I told them as long as we did well at district concert band festival, then they could have marching band in the spring. So we would march in the fall, and then we would stop from December all the way through district festival. After district festival, I would let them do some marching in the spring. As long as they gave me what I wanted, I was fine, and they did it. You have to set goals for students, and they will rise to whatever, if you encourage them and motivate them. They love traveling. They and their parents love to travel, and therefore, they'll work hard. We went to Beijing a few years back, and were in London, England this last year at the same time that the Olympics were being held.

When we were performing in London, something wonderful happened. We performed two nights at Windsor Castle, and as we were performing, the crowd grew. The first night it was maybe 100 people. The second night there must have been 300, and they were just astounded by the marching band. They had never seen anything like it. They just loved us. One night, our travel agent came and sat next to me on the bus. He said, you won't believe this. He told me that somebody has called the Olympic committee, and they want your band to come and play at the Olympics. They want you to march around the Olympic Park and play. And there were tears in my eyes. We played at the Olympic Park and it was just a dream come true, and thousands and thousands and thousands of people saw us play. I didn't go to the Olympics as an athlete, but I got to go as a band director. That was the highlight of my career so far.

CHAPTER 2
Understanding Our Students

Equipped with an open, informed, and positive perspective on urban music education, we can move forward to the important task of better understanding the students we teach. Although our focus as music educators is on providing a comprehensive music education for our students, there are other, important aspects of our students' lives that we need to know and understand. Among them is often the existence of a sizable opportunity gap between urban students and their peers in other school settings. In this chapter, I begin with an overview of research related to this "opportunity gap," followed by a discussion of the important concepts of race, ethnicity, and socioeconomic status.

THE OPPORTUNITY GAP

Too often there are problematic gaps in achievement between student populations in urban schools and their peers in other settings. Researchers Kevin Welner and Prudence Carter (2013) have noted that

> the persistent test score gaps in our schools include those between African Americans and Whites, between Latinos and Whites, between students in poverty and wealthier students, between children of parents with little formal education and with greater formal education, and between English learners and native English speakers. . . . Similar gaps exist for other important outcomes, such as rates of high school and college graduation. (pp. 2–3)

As urban teachers who care a great deal about maximizing the success of our students, we can be disheartened when we hear about these achievement gaps. However, as Welner and Carter point out, the modern day political and educational policy focus on gaps in *achievement* tends to obscure the existence of significant documented disparities in educational and economic *opportunity* between student groups according to skin color, ethnicity, language, and social class status. These disparities of opportunity include such important factors as "health, housing, nutrition, safety, and enriching experiences, in addition to opportunities provided through formal elementary and secondary school preparation" (2013, p. 3). Milner (2010) states:

> I believe a focus on an achievement gap places too much blame and emphasis on students themselves as individuals and not enough attention on why gaps and disparities are commonplace in schools across the country. Opportunity, on the other hand, forces us to think about how systems, processes, and institutions are overtly and covertly designed to maintain the status quo and sustain depressingly complicated disparities in education. (p. 8)

Indeed, Irvine (2010) suggests that the perceived "achievement gap" is simply a result of other gaps that exist in modern education, such as

> the teacher quality gap, the teacher training gap, the challenging curriculum gap, the school funding gap, the digital divide gap, the wealth and income gap, the employment opportunity gap, the affordable housing gap, the health care gap, the nutrition gap, the school integration gap, and the quality childcare gap." (p. xii)

The achievement "gap" that is noticed in student test scores, then, does not imply that something is "wrong" with students of color and other under-achieving groups. Instead, it may reveal that something is wrong with the opportunities and resources that they have been provided.

In the United States, public school is often viewed as being the "great equalizer"—a common resource provided to level the playing field for all children. Although differences in the availability of resources within schools that serve different communities have been frequently noted (Kozol, 1991), the inequalities that face children *before* they enter school are often overlooked. For example, Lee and Burkam (2002, p. 2) found the following in a large-scale study of a nationally representative sample of kindergarten students:

- Before entering kindergarten, the average cognitive score of children in the highest socioeconomic (SES) group is 60 percent above the scores of the lowest SES group.
- Race and ethnicity are strongly associated with socioeconomic status, and differences in test scores between students of different races are apparent even in kindergarten. However, the differences in performance by race and ethnicity can be substantially explained by other variables, such as SES, family educational expectations, access to quality childcare, home reading, computer use, and television habits. Of all of these variables, "SES accounts for more of the unique variation in cognitive scores than any other factor by far."
- Lower SES children begin school at kindergarten in substantially lower-quality elementary schools than their better-resourced counterparts, in terms of higher student achievement, more school resources, more qualified teachers, more positive teacher attitudes, and better neighborhood or school conditions. This reinforces the inequalities that develop even before children reach school age.

Indeed, the opportunity gap may result not only from a lack of resources but also from differences in foundational experiences within society. For example, Lareau (2011) found many commonalities in the ways that both lower-income and higher-income parents raise their children. However, she found striking differences in the ways that children were prepared to interact successfully with institutional structures (such as those found in schools) according to social class (defined by the parents' level of education and the family's income). In her study, children of highly formally educated and high-income parents exhibited substantially more involvement in organized activities from a younger age than did children of less well-educated and lower-income parents, giving them an early "edge" when it comes to learning the norms and rules of the school or institutional structure.

Understanding the opportunity gap allows us to reject many of the stereotypes and deficit language that we as urban teachers so frequently hear. Differences found between cultural groups in standardized test performance may obscure some very important inequalities within our system of education:

> In America's meritocratic culture, the idea of a competition implies both fair play and deserved outcomes. The culture suggests that people . . . study hard in college and are rewarded with good jobs, where they continue to conscientiously apply themselves and, thus, accrue more and bigger rewards. But the fact that many middle-class youth work hard should not blind us to the underlying reality that the system is not fair. It is not neutral. It does not give all children equal opportunities. Not only do schools vary, but in schools and other institutions that sort children into positions in the stratification system, some cultural practices are simply privileged more than others. Our culture's nearly exclusive focus on individual choices renders invisible the key role of institutions. In America, social class backgrounds frame and transform individual actions. The life paths we pursue, thus, are neither equal nor freely chosen. (Laureau, 2011, p. 343).

TEACHING, LEARNING, AND THE "CULTURE OF POWER"

All educators hold certain expectations for their students, and for their behavior in particular, that likely originate in their own upbringing. Rules such as expectations for eye contact, strategies for the diffusion of tension, appropriate uses of humor, and guidelines for when it's appropriate to speak and when it's appropriate to stay silent are often "hidden" in our classrooms—that is, we do not usually explicitly post these rules on our walls or describe them to our students. Instead, we just assume that others will hold the same values for particular behaviors that we do:

> What constitutes acceptable behavior and appropriate discipline for students at home can be significantly different from the discipline and rules of behavior experienced in the classroom. Normal classroom behavior can be informed by different cultural frames, such as race, socioeconomics, language, or even geography. (Milner, 2010, p. 25)

Educators often misinterpret actions and behaviors within the classroom as being defiant or oppositional, when they are not intended as such. For example, Milner provides the example of a student who is used to "joking around" with family members when a conflict arises. Indeed, such joking may be seen as very welcome strategy within the family unit, as a means to de-escalate the situation or avoid a confrontation. A teacher, on the other hand, may consider this use of humor in the classroom rude and inappropriate, leading to a cultural conflict within the classroom. The teacher may also see this behavior as a challenge to his or her authority. The student is therefore punished for using a strategy that has been proven successful in his or her own home setting. See the next sidebar, Beyond First Glance, for examples of the ways that our panel has worked to ease tension with students.

Lisa Delpit has coined the term "culture of power" to describe the often hidden rules that educators and administrators expect students to follow in schools. Delpit describes this as follows:

> (a) issues of power are enacted in classrooms; (b) there are codes or rules for participating in power; that is, there is a "culture of power"; (c) the rules of the culture of power are a reflection of the rules of the culture of those who have power; (d) if you are not already a participant in the culture of power, being told explicitly the rules of that culture makes acquiring power easier; and (e) those with power are frequently least aware of—or least willing to acknowledge—its existence. Those with less power are often most aware of its existence. (Delpit, 1995, p. 24)

According to Delpit, educators must make attempts to overtly articulate the "rules" of the classroom and the consequences for breaking them. Milner (2010) agrees:

> For students to have a chance at success in the classroom, and thus in society, they must understand that they live in a system that can be oppressive and repressive. . . . Students almost always lose what I have come to call "cultural

SIDEBAR: BEYOND FIRST GLANCE

Ramon

You have to remember that they sometimes have a bad day, too. They have problems at home, and they sometimes take it out on you. You have to realize that, okay, they're going through this, and it's my job to help. Sometimes I go, "Are you okay today?" They say, well, my Mom yelled at me and said this and that. And so . . . okay. That's why. I say, "I got you." And sometimes, as the teacher, you think it's your fault. They're not improving because of me. They don't care. But the reason why you're teaching is because you love kids and you want kids to be successful, so you have to keep at it. We're here in this profession to change kids' lives.

Martha

I think something that young teachers frequently do, as I did, is to label those kids as "bad," and not really see that there's a very different kid behind that behavior that really needs somebody to see beyond what they are putting out. I had a fifth grader this year who has special needs and who was notorious in the school. Everybody knew this kid, as he was always in trouble, especially in the younger years. He was labeled as a "bad" kid. But he had probably the best voice of any student I've ever had. So when we found that out, that was a pathway in . . . The fact that he could get up on the stage and sing, and his family could come and see him do something positive instead of all these negatives, that was a huge thing. With a kid like that, your instinct may be to sort of push back and try and clamp down on him, but maybe he's a kid who, if you challenge him, it's going to be worse than to walk away from the behavior. So that takes time to figure that out. Every kid's different.

Deanna

Every night when I go home, my job is to figure it out what could I be doing to better reach this child, or, how can I get other people in my building to really understand where this kid is coming from. Teachers sometimes come to me who have negative things to say about certain students, and I just can't agree with that. My question is always "what are you doing to make this a better situation for yourself?"

Eric

There is a young man in my program who is one of the "cool cats" in class. His brother was involved in gangs and was shot and killed, and because of all that he had been through, he had a sort of "rough and tough" exterior. But he was a really, really incredibly smart, sweet, thoughtful young man. You would never see that from him in a large group setting. The way I learned more about him was just in little one on one conversations before and after class, just a kind word here and there, a question about his weekend, asking if he needed help with any of his subjects. He eventually warmed up to me, as he did to some other staff in our department. Everyone else in the building worried that he was going to end up dead or in jail. And they really missed out on the really fine qualities that he possessed. I think it's difficult to look past that rough exterior sometimes, but I think we just have to push to get past that with every student at every opportunity.

Victoria

I believe that students often act in a certain way because things are wrong at home. Maybe there's a divorce going on, or maybe they're being abused in some kind of way. I'll talk to another teacher and they'll say, well, this person acts up in my room. And I'll give them maybe a hint of what the child is going through at home and I'll talk with the child so that they'll do better. But if you were 16 years old today and you looked at the world and you saw all these people without jobs: engineers, people who work in the factory, and even teachers, if you're 16 years old or 15, why in the world would you keep on going to school? These other people went to school. They got college degrees. They were working for years, and they have nothing. People are losing jobs and homes, and it's in these children's minds. And they're like, why should I even do this? Why should I care? Why should I work hard? It's hard because, as a teacher, you sometimes get vulnerable because it seems like they are trying to hurt you. But it's not that they try to hurt you. High school students, no matter what, just like teenagers at home, they feel like they know more than you. When your children get to be 16 to 17 years old, they're going to feel like you're stupid and they're smarter than you no matter how many degrees you have. It just happens.

battles" in the classroom—mainly because students do not necessarily think, act, and live as their teachers do or as their teachers' biological children do. In short, it is irresponsible and simply unfair to expect students to behave in a way that has not been well explained to them. Teachers should not assume that students understand the culture of power; teachers must teach it! (p. 26)

While educators should help students understand the hidden rules related to the "culture of power," it is simultaneously important to encourage students to question its existence. Many students will encounter conflict between their own culture and the "culture of power" throughout their lives. Being able to thoughtfully question power dynamics (Who is making the rules in this situation, and why have they been afforded the power to do so? Where do I fit in within this system? Does this system represent a just distribution of power, and, if not, how can it be changed?) provides students with a framework for navigating such situations throughout their lives.

CONSIDERING RACE, ETHNICITY, AND SOCIOECONOMIC STATUS

There are many aspects of our students' background and characteristics that are important to consider, but here I discuss three that tend to be mentioned with frequency by urban educators: race, ethnicity, and socioeconomic status. Trying to consider the role of each of these in our own and our students' lives is important, but they are frequently misunderstood. It is important to realize that the terminology associated with race, ethnicity, and socioeconomic status has changed frequently in past years and is likely to continue changing. If you are ever confused about what terminology to use with your students, parents, or colleagues, Sonia Nieto (2004) suggests two helpful criteria:

1. What do the people themselves want to be called?
2. What is the most accurate term? (p. 25)

Race

The concept of race is an important one for teachers to consider and understand, especially given the history and importance of race relations in the United States. First, it is important to understand that, as Sonia Nieto (2000) points out, the concept of race, in a strictly biological sense, does not exist at all: "There is no scientific evidence that so-called racial groups differ biologically or genetically in significant ways. Differences that do exist are primarily social; that is, they are based on one's experiences within a particular cultural group" (p. 27). However, the concept of race as it has been historically constructed is significant, in that this particular concept has been used to "oppress entire groups of people for their supposed differences" (p. 27).

Because educational opportunities and outcomes in the United States vary tremendously among students of different races (Bluestone,

Stevenson, & Williams, 2008; Orfield et al., 2004), it is important that music teachers consider and acknowledge issues of race. Despite this, many well-meaning teachers continue to state that they are "color-blind" or that they "do not see color" within their classrooms. This attitude toward race is problematic, according to Gloria Ladson-Billings (1994):

> Given the significance of race and color in American society, it is impossible to believe that a classroom teacher does not notice the race and ethnicity of the children she is teaching. Further, by claiming not to notice, the teacher is saying that she is dismissing one of the most salient features of the child's identity and that she does not account for it in her curricular planning and instruction. Saying we are aware of students' race and ethnic background is not the same as saying we treat students inequitably. . . . If teachers pretend not to see students' racial and ethnic differences, they are limited in their ability to meet their educational needs. (p. 33)

Similarly, according to Milner:

> too many educators gloss over race as an important area of consideration in broader diversity discussions, for a variety of reasons: (1) They are uncomfortable talking about it, (2) they find it irrelevant to do so, (3) race is sometimes considered a taboo subject due to its horrific history for some in U.S. society, and (4) race is misunderstood by so many, both within and outside of education. (Milner, 2010, p. 7).

Acknowledging the role of race in our society allows us to recognize institutionalized disparities and inequities in educational settings, such as these:

- An overrepresentation of students of color in special education
- An underrepresentation of students of color in gifted education
- An over-referral of African American students to the office for disciplinary actions and consequences
- An overwhelming number of African American students who are expelled or suspended
- An underrepresentation of students of color in school-wide clubs, organizations, and other prestigious arenas, such as the school's homecoming court and student government
- An underrepresentation of faculty and staff of color in school positions, including professional staff, teaching, and leadership positions (Milner, 2010, p. 22)

To this list, I might also add an underrepresentation of students of color in music performance ensembles. In particular, in an analysis of national enrollment in school music ensembles, Elpus and Abril (2011) found these groups underrepresented: Hispanic students, students in the lowest quartile of socioeconomic status, native Spanish speakers, and students whose parents had earned a high school diploma or less.

To overcome these racial inequalities and prepare all students (including White students) to thrive in a multiracial society, Tatum (2007) suggests a multifaceted approach that she calls the "ABC's": *affirming* identity, *building* community, and *cultivating* leadership:

> A, affirming identity, refers to the fact that students need to see themselves—important dimensions of their identity—reflected in the environment around them, in the curriculum, among faculty and staff, and in the faces of their classmates, to voice the feelings of invisibility or marginality that can undermine student success. B, building community, refers to the importance of creating a school community in which everyone has a sense of belonging, a community in which there are shared norms and values as well as a sense of common purpose that unites its members. C, cultivating leadership, refers to the role of education in preparing citizens for active participation in a democracy, and the assumption that leadership must come from all parts of our community. Leadership in the twenty-first century requires the ability to interact effectively with people from backgrounds different from one's own—an ability that requires real-life experience. (p. 22)

Ethnicity

Ethnicity differs in important ways from race. For example, as Sonia Nieto points out, "African Americans and Haitians are both Black. They share some basic cultural values and are both subjected to racist attitudes and behaviors in the United States. But the particular experiences, native language use, and ethnicity of each group is overlooked or even denied if we simply call them both Black rather than also identifying them ethnically" (p. 27). Nieto says that White people seldom think of themselves as ethnic—a term that is often reserved for

> other, more easily identifiable groups. Nevertheless, the fact is that we are all ethnic, whether we choose to identify ourselves in this way or not. . . . Although Whiteness is an important factor, it hides more than it reveals: There is a tremendous diversity of ethnic backgrounds among Whites, and this is lost if race is the only identifier. (Nieto, 2000, p. 26)

Similarly, the terms Latino(a) and Hispanic are commonly used to refer to people of Latin American or Caribbean heritage. However, many Latino(a) students prefer to identify as being members of more specific cultural communities, such as being Puerto Rican, Mexican, Mexican American, Dominican, or Salvadoran. The differences between these cultural groups can be profound; indeed, the native language of some Guatemalans is not Spanish, and many Dominicans have an African background (Nieto, 2000). The same can be said for students who are often referred to as Asian American but would prefer to identify as, for example, Chinese, Japanese, Vietnamese, Filipino, or Native Hawaiian. For us as music teachers, exploring our students' ethnicity can often uncover musical traditions that could be shared within our classrooms. Because music is an important part of almost all cultures, we should see the ethnic background of our students as an important resource within our classroom.

We must also remember that many students within our schools may have limited English language proficiency. As a teacher who is sensitively attuned to your students' needs, you will want to find ways to support their language growth while providing numerous opportunities for musical success within your classroom. More resources on assisting English language learning (ELL) students can be found in Chapter 6. In the following list, I paraphrase Carlos Abril's (2003) helpful suggestions for music teachers looking to better support English language learning students in the music classroom:

1. *Show respect:* We need to foster positive experiences for our ELL students, being sensitive to include them in as many musical activities as possible, and sometimes offering them adapted nonverbal musical opportunities so as not to force them into activities for which they are expected to speak English.
2. *Get students involved:* Talk with your English language learning students via a school translator or another child who speaks the language in order to learn about their past experiences with music and to understand any challenges that they may be facing in your school. Maintain high expectations while understanding the complexity of learning both language and musical content at the same time. Allow opportunities for cooperative learning with peers.
3. *Study the culture:* Consider including aspects of your students' culture in the music curriculum, and work to select songs and experiences that respectfully depict the students' culture.
4. *Promote a safe learning environment:* Understand that most ELL students go through an initial phase of refusing to talk with teachers or peers. When ELL students do speak in music class, refrain from publicly correcting their pronunciation, and provide abundant praise when they make an effort to speak in English.
5. *Foster students' musical learning:* Use hand signs to represent certain musical terms or concepts, look for songs that use repetition, select some songs that use nonsense syllables, and have students learn songs on a neutral syllable before adding words. (pp. 40-43)

As we work to assist multilingual students in the music classroom, it is also important to be aware that these English language learners may have very sophisticated linguistic skills in their native language or even in multiple languages. Rather than focus on what these students do not yet know in English, we can focus on providing the resources within our classroom that will help them build on their existing strengths and prior knowledge.

It is important that we as teachers work hard to understand and know our students. The next sidebar, Getting to Know Your Students, can provide examples of ways to do so.

SIDEBAR: GETTING TO KNOW YOUR STUDENTS

HOW DO YOU FIND WAYS TO GET TO KNOW YOUR STUDENTS?

Ramon

I work hard to know a lot about the students, including their families—the mom, the dad, the sister, the brother. I have a lot of siblings in the mariachi program, and we get to know them. We become a very important relationship person in the community, and the students get to feel like it's their second home when they're in our class. I get to know them because I ask the students. I have them do a lot of surveys. I ask them, what do you like about this program? What is your favorite part of this year? How have you grown? What song do you like to play? I ask these things just so I can have that feedback, because you don't have time to interview all the kids. You don't. You don't, but with their written feedback, it kind of tells you about them, what you have accomplished, and things you need to work on.

Martha

One of the first things I do is survey my students. I just get up and ask them questions and have them respond, and then I read all their answers about what music they listen to, what TV they watch, what kind of families they come from. I also do a lot of work in the beginning with family—where, what—because I am fascinated with the ethnic diversity of being in this New York school. I do a lot of activities to find out their cultural background and all that kind of stuff. I still always try and find new ways to know them better. When you're seeing them once a week, you just don't get the amount of time you'd like.

Deanna

It's important in any teaching environment to take the time to understand that each person is unique. I do a lot of transporting students, so I know where my students live. I'm pretty involved in my students' lives and try to make things happen for them. Outside of the classroom, I try to touch base with people, especially if there's a feeling that there's a negative energy between us, which happens. I try to make sure when I see them in the hallway that I give them just a smile or something or a hug—anything like that can make things better.

Eric

I spend an inordinate amount of time getting to know them at the beginning of the year, especially with my beginners. Of course, we start doing music right away. But every day, we do something to get to know each other. My smallest classes are like 75 students, so it can be a challenge to get to know everybody. But they have to know each other, and they have to know me, and I have to know them. We spend lots of time with trust building games or team building games and activities that help them understand that we're all on the same page, and that we all have these wonderful shared experiences. At the same time, there's this tremendous diversity among us, despite the fact that 90 percent of them are Mexican immigrants. We talk about how to respect that diversity and why we are here, and they give lots of reflection on those things, too. I spend a lot of time at the beginning of the year getting to know my students, and that continues throughout the year.

Victoria

In my program, we spend a lot of time together after school. We do fundraising, and I work with the children on the weekends. I also take some time for socializing with them and doing leadership training. Everybody also has to say hello to me when they come in the room every day. So, I spend a lot of one-on-one time with my students. I'll have small groups of leaders and officers over to my house, where we'll watch a leadership development video together. I do depend on them. I think that's one of the things that music does—we have our students at least one, two, three, or four years. We have a chance to get to know them and watch them evolve, so that's very important to me. My program is not just about music. It's about building people, and when you build people, you have a great band. When you have children who believe in themselves and learn to trust others and work with others, then you have a more successful program. So, if I see a kid who looks troubled, either I talk to them, I have a student talk to them, or I try and get a parent to listen to them, because they need to talk to somebody. You can prevent so many problems if you address a face.

Socioeconomic Status

The term "socioeconomic status" is a complex concept consisting of two interrelated aspects of a person's background: one that includes resources, such as education, income, and wealth, and the other that includes status or rank as a function of relative position in a hierarchy, such as social class (Krieger, Williams, & Moss, 1997). The poverty rates in urban areas are, in most cases, much higher than those in suburban areas, and the proportion of people living in poverty in urban areas is greater today than it was in the 1960s and 1970s (Bluestone, Stevenson, & Williams, 2008, p. 49). Because family income is highly correlated with education (p. 53), this is especially important for urban educators to consider.

Historically, educators have disagreed about the ways socioeconomic status, and poverty in particular, can be understood. For years, educational authors wrote about the concept of a "culture of poverty"—the idea that poor people share many similar characteristics, including beliefs, values, and behaviors. In reality, differences in values and beliefs among poor people are just as wide as among middle- and upper-class people. The "culture of poverty" narrative has led to many misunderstandings about individuals living with fewer financial resources. Paul Gorski (2008, p. 32) has highlighted four of these myths:

1. MYTH: Poor people are unmotivated and have weak work ethics.
    The Reality: Poor people do not have weaker work ethics or lower levels of motivation than wealthier people (Iversen & Farber, 1996; Wilson, 1997). . . . According to the Economic Policy Institute (2002), poor working adults spend more hours working each week than their wealthier counterparts.
2. MYTH: Poor parents are uninvolved in their children's learning, largely because they do not value education.
    The Reality: Low-income parents hold the same attitudes about education that wealthy parents do (Compton-Lilly, 2003; Lareau & Horvat, 1999; Leichter, 1978). Low-income parents . . . are more likely to work multiple jobs, to work evenings, to have jobs without paid leave, and to be unable to afford child care and public transportation.
3. MYTH: Poor people are linguistically deficient.
    The Reality: All people, regardless of the languages and language varieties they speak, use a full continuum of language registers (Bomer, Dworin, May, & Semingson, 2008). . . . What often are assumed to be deficient varieties of English (Appalachian varieties, perhaps, or what some refer to as Black English Vernacular) are no less sophisticated than so-called standard English.

4. MYTH: Poor people tend to abuse drugs and alcohol.

The Reality: Poor people are no more likely than their wealthier counterparts to abuse alcohol or drugs. Although drug sales are more visible in poor neighborhoods, drug use is equally distributed across poor, middle-class, and wealthy communities (Saxe, Kadushin, Tighe, Rindskopf, & Beveridge, 2001). Chen, Sheth, Krejci, and Wallace (2003) found that alcohol consumption is significantly higher among upper-middle-class white high school students than among poor black high school students. Their finding supports a history of research showing that alcohol abuse is far more prevalent among wealthy people than among poor people. (Diala, Muntaner, & Walrath, 2004; Galea, Ahern, Tracy, & Vlahov, 2007)

The issue of socioeconomic status may be especially relevant to music programs, as cuts in music program funding often result in music students having to pay special fees in addition to the traditional expenses of renting/purchasing instruments and purchasing music and equipment when they are not provided by the school. Unfortunately, the best predictors of the availability of music programs at the middle and high school levels are socioeconomic status and school size (C. Smith, 1997). These inequities among and within music programs are real and problematic, as Vincent Bates (2012) has observed:

> School music, in particular, poses an array of added expenses that could contribute to unequal access and achievement. Families may not be able to afford musical instruments and accessories, instrument repair and maintenance, performance attire, private lessons, or transportation to and from special events. Single parents or those who work evenings will have less time to monitor and encourage music practice at home or to attend concerts. Lack of dental or medical care could affect students' abilities or desires to play wind instruments or to sign up for school choirs. (p. 34)

When talking with the teachers featured in this book, I found that all of them had used their own personal funds to help students do things such as buy food, clothing, computers, pay fees, and afford to attend music camps or other musical activities. Each discussed the tremendous effect that low socioeconomic status had on many of their students. Eric, for example, talked about the impact of poverty for his students on the South side of Chicago:

> A lot of my students don't get enough to eat. They have difficulty with bus fares, so we find ways to support them to get to and from school, or to sing in an outside ensemble. Sometimes we find them scholarships to a local music program,

and we work to find the resources to get them there. The level of instability in some of my students' homes, to me, was staggering to see. I grew up in a very stable home with a very stable environment. I lived in one house my entire life. Our school has a 35 percent mobility rate. So, it's a big challenge.

As a new urban teacher, I didn't understand that the unspoken reason many of my students could not attend after-school rehearsals or other musical activities was because they needed to go to work to help contribute to the family's finances or babysit younger siblings while their parents worked a second or third job. Students are often ashamed or embarrassed to talk about a lack of resources, so we need to be responsive to and respectful of their needs. Other important issues related to socioeconomic status include homelessness and student transience/mobility, which can greatly affect a student's ability to learn in our classrooms. When we identify students who may be experiencing these issues or are otherwise in need of support, it is important that we recognize the important role that school staff such as counselors, school psychologists, school nurses, and social workers can play in assisting our students.

Race, ethnicity, and socioeconomic status are just three of many important issues that we need to consider with regard to our students' needs. These three important variables are often related to the opportunity gap that so many of our students experience due to pervasive and systematic inequities. While we focus on providing a comprehensive music education for our students, we must also be sure to remain informed about aspects of our students' lives and experiences that affect their learning.

CHAPTER 3

Contextually Specific Music Teaching

An Introduction

Most of us decided to become a teacher because we wanted to work with children and young adults in some way. Even the most disillusioned and hardened of teachers will usually admit to entering the profession because he or she loved working with children through music. However, the complex nature of music teaching and the many demands of the music classroom often cause us to focus our energies on other, less important aspects of the job (purchase orders, instrument inventories, and curriculum rewrites, anyone?). In so doing, we are often pulled away from the single most important focus of our profession: that of improving and enriching the lives of young people through music.

A teacher must have a fundamental understanding of each student's background, family of origin, culture, and particular strengths, weaknesses, and interests if he or she is to be successful. Working across grade levels and within larger ensembles, music teachers often teach more students than the typical classroom teacher (and sometimes see them only once or twice a week!); this can make getting to know our students somewhat more difficult. From another view, we often teach the same students for several years, and we engage with them in many activities outside the school day, which can give us greater opportunities for relationship-building than some other teachers have (Edgar, 2012).

As Bernstein commented: "If the culture of the teacher is to become part of the consciousness of the child, the culture of the child must first be in the consciousness of the teacher" (Bernstein, 1970, p. 115). This specialized knowledge of students, school settings, and school communities is referred to by researchers as a teacher's "knowledge of context" (Grossman, 1990). It is an essential component of a teacher's understanding of the teaching and learning process, and is necessary for success in any setting. According to researcher Pamela Grossman (1990), "teachers' knowledge, to be of use for classroom practice, must be context-specific, that is, it must be adapted to their specific students and the demands of their districts" (p. 9). Thus, we can't successfully teach music in precisely the same way in different settings and with different students; good teachers understand that all learning takes place in a particular context and is best accomplished when the needs and experiences of learners are aligned with the goals and techniques of the teacher:

> Teachers teach the same content in different ways to different students. Indeed, an individual teacher is faced with a particular curriculum and a particular group of students, located in a particular school. . . . In other words, the teacher's classroom decisions are located in, and contingent upon, a specific social, cultural, and educational context. (Barnett and Hodson, 2001, p. 433)

Our greatest opportunity for improving the types of educational experiences that we provide students lies in taking the time to better understand who they are, what they know, and how we can tailor our curriculum and pedagogy to meet their needs. Even if you've taught at the same school for years, your students have likely changed quite a bit during your tenure. It's time for us to take a fresh look at our students.

NURTURING THE DEVELOPMENT OF ALL OF OUR STUDENTS[1]

As students begin formal schooling, they form opinions concerning their abilities, due in large part to how well they can assimilate culturally into the school environment. The cultural messages that students receive in school settings can greatly affect their subsequent achievement. In the words of Sonia Nieto, "Student performance is based on both overt and covert messages from teachers about students' worth, intelligence, and capability" (2000, p. 43). In many music classrooms, students come from a variety of cultures and circumstances, and they differ in terms of race, gender, religion, ethnicity, socioeconomic status, exceptionality,[2] and sexual orientation. All of these differences affect the ability of children to make connections between their personal identity and the school music curriculum.

The identity development of students of differing cultural backgrounds can be markedly different (Negy, Shreve, Benson, & Uddin, 2004), and research can help us understand how our students' identities are formed. For example, researcher William Cross has studied the development of racial identity in African Americans. He has written that the self-concept of African American students depends heavily on their reference group orientation, or how well they feel that their own personal identity as an African American aligns with the norms and expectations of the culture that surrounds them (Cross, 1971). How does this apply to the music classroom? When a student sees, for instance, that the music that he or she enjoys and values at home or with friends is ignored or degraded by institutions such as schools, it creates cultural conflict. By authentically aligning our music curriculum

---

1. The sections entitled "Nurturing the Development of All of our Students" and "Considering Culturally Relevant Pedagogy within the Music Classroom" are excerpted with permission from the author's 2012 article in the *Music Educators Journal* (Fitzpatrick, 2012).

2. "Exceptionality" refers to cognitive, physical, social, or behavioral differences of students within a large spectrum of ability.

with the music that our students value, we can find better ways to connect more effectively with their personal identities. When this happens, our students' perception of conflict is lessened, resulting in an improved self-concept. Cross's model provides an explanation of the challenges that African American students may face when navigating cultural boundaries, but it can also be understood as helping us understand the needs of students from various cultural backgrounds.

What can we do as teachers to lessen the identity conflicts that our students might experience between the classroom and home? There are several important conditions that we can help promote within the boundaries of our classrooms and schools. For example, the following have been found to be important factors in reducing student racial and cultural identity conflicts and encouraging academic success:

1. Positive peer relationships with members of the same cultural group;
2. Knowledge about the notable achievements of members of the same cultural group;
3. The availability of role models;
4. The encouragement of significant adults. (Tatum, 2004)

How can we better foster such conditions within our music classrooms? First, we can pay more attention to the social interactions of our students and develop curricula that allow for positive peer interactions to develop, paying special attention to the cultural background of our students when grouping them for projects and assignments. We can also include within our curriculum pieces composed, performed, and arranged by musicians who reflect the cultural background of our students, and we can discuss the contributions that these individuals have made to music history and contemporary society. In sharing profound musical experiences with our students, we often serve as role models. We need to be aware of the commonalities we share with our students and use these to help us connect with them (see sidebar, Bringing Our Background into the Foreground). However, if we do not have the same racial, ethnic, or cultural background as our students, we might wish to bring into our classrooms artists, musicians, and guests who reflect our students' cultural identities to serve as role models.

Finally, as teachers who frequently play significant roles in the lives of our students, we can be proactive in recognizing the unique potential of each individual, regardless of cultural background. Students may excel in different ways in our classrooms than they do elsewhere in the school or community.

SIDEBAR: BRINGING OUR BACKGROUND INTO THE FOREGROUND

CONSIDERING OUR OWN BACKGROUND AND WHAT WE SHARE WITH OUR STUDENTS

Ramon

I'm very lucky that I'm bilingual and bi-cultural and have that opportunity to relate to the students. I think that the students see the work ethic that I show, and I hope that they learn that being a minority you have to be twice as good and be willing to work twice as hard. They see that I have to work twice as hard and be twice as good as any teacher in any other program because this is life. In life, you have to work your hardest, and teaching them that work ethic is important to me. If you want something, don't ask for it—earn it, just like when we want uniforms, we sell popcorn and we have fundraisers and hustle so that we can get what we need. Hard work pays off. What they need is a good role model. Sometimes they don't have that at home because their families are always working.

Martha

My school and community is so diverse, and I am from small-town America. During standardized testing early in my career, they gave me three or four kids that could not be tested because they did not speak a word of English, and my job was to sit with them during the test. I didn't speak any of their languages, and they were all different. They spoke four different languages. So what I did was I had a CD of music from all kinds of different countries and I just put it on and I told them to draw. I kind of got the message across to tell them to just draw what they heard in the music. It was amazing to watch each kid, as the music for their country came on, just light up like a Christmas tree. All of a sudden, they wanted to go to the map and they wanted to show me where their country was. They were trying so hard to tell me about their country and their family and everything. That was pretty profound experience for me of how music is powerful even when you don't share language.

Deanna

I've never doubted my choice of where I teach because it's part of my community, it's where I grew up and it's my home. I went though the Detroit schools myself as a minority in that system: as a White student. I really don't feel this now because it's my home and this is my family, but at times, I did feel like I had a chip on my shoulder. I felt that I had to prove to people in my community that, oh, yeah. I graduated from the Detroit Public Schools in '86, so they could see me as part of this community.

Eric

My race and ethnic background and my upbringing are completely different to who my students are and what they see in their communities. I don't feel like it has presented challenges to me—I feel like it's presented me with opportunities. One of the first things I did when I got the job is I moved into the neighborhood, and it's a really rough neighborhood. Our school is not especially rough—we have great kids, but the neighborhood is pretty rough. I moved into the neighborhood because I was like, hey, look, if I'm going to be teaching here, I have to know about this community. I have to know who these people are. I have to know what makes them tick and what their families look like and what they see. For me, that was just a really basic fundamental first step in getting to know my students and their experience. Even living in the neighborhood, it took me two or three years before I felt like I really understood what was happening in their lives and in the school and in the community. One of the things I tell my students all the time is what my experiences were like when I was their age and what my community and especially what my school was like—and they're stunned. They're floored. They can't imagine something so extravagant and well-resourced and supported. I tell them that the reason I'm here is that I believe that you deserve that same thing. I feel like any expectations of the type of education that I received have been crushed out of them, if they've gone through the Chicago Public School system. And so it's important for me to share where I came from to them because it helps them understand a little bit about me and why I'm there, despite the fact that our experiences were so different.

Victoria

I think children can read adults very well, and they know when you're phony. Whether you're Black or White or yellow, they know when you're for real. They know if you care. They can read people, and they mistreat Black teachers and they'll mistreat White teachers. But some people, they don't mistreat them because they know those people are for real and they care about them and they really want to teach them. Children can read adults. So, you can teach anywhere if you really love to teach. Now, if you're teaching somewhere because you can't get another job or you're teaching just so you can get that insurance and you can have some money, children will read that. They know if you're for real. They're going to always try you no matter what, but it's your attitude and the way you respond to them when they try you that matters.

CONSIDERING CULTURALLY RELEVANT PEDAGOGY
WITHIN THE MUSIC CLASSROOM

Through professional development workshops, undergraduate or graduate courses in education, or books and articles on urban teaching, you may have become familiar with the concept of culturally relevant pedagogy. If you have not yet come across this concept, I strongly recommend that you read Gloria Ladson-Billings's book *The Dreamkeepers* (1994). Although she focuses on teaching African American students, Ladson-Billings presents the topic of culturally relevant pedagogy in ways that apply to many of our students. Basically, culturally relevant pedagogy embraces the establishment of natural ties between in-school work and out-of-school experiences as a means of decreasing the disconnect that many students feel between these two worlds. It came about because research indicates that many students are becoming increasingly alienated from traditional means of schooling, failing to see the relevance between their home lives and their school environments (Hayes, 1993; Washington, 1989). Culturally relevant pedagogy is often cited as a way that teachers might increase student investment in and comprehension of school curricula (Ensign, 2003). Culturally relevant teaching is

> a pedagogy that empowers students intellectually, socially, emotionally, and politically, by using cultural referents to impart knowledge, skills, and attitudes. These cultural references are not merely vehicles for bridging or explaining the dominant culture; they are aspects of the curriculum in their own right. (Ladson-Billings, 17-18)

In the field of music education, where creativity and personal expression are valued, it is especially important to address the disconnect that students may perceive between home and school cultures.

Culturally Relevant Pedagogy: The Content

One way that music teachers can better connect in-school and out-of-school experiences is by focusing on the content of the curriculum. For music teachers, including music within the curriculum that represents different cultural traditions must begin with an inquiry into the multiple cultures that students might represent, as a student's cultural identity and heritage may not be readily apparent and indeed may differ quite significantly from his or her obvious skin color and physical characteristics. Learning more about students' cultural backgrounds could take place in many ways across general music, band, choir, and orchestra settings, as students are encouraged to "tell their own story" of the multiple cultures that they represent.

Once teachers better understand these multiple cultures, they can be creative about the ways that they include music within the classroom. For example, one general music teacher, Leanne (Robinson, 2006), made trips to students' homes to experience firsthand the songs and dances of their heritage, which she then brought to the classroom. Leanne even invited parents into the school to perform these traditional dances and songs. Leanne described her goals as follows:

> My dream is to finally get such a repertoire that no matter what country somebody comes from, we have something that would go—You're from this country and on their first day in class you take out the video and you play it for them and they are like—"Oh, there's a piece of home that I get right here, and maybe this place isn't so horrible," because we deal with the culture shock thing so drastically. (p. 41)

Teachers can also help make explicit connections between schoolwork and students' lives by exploring the musical cultures and traditions of the local communities that surround the school. Indeed, researcher Victor Bobetsky (2005) described a choir director's effort to increase student understanding of the African American culture within a Brooklyn community. In this project, a choir director in Brooklyn partnered with other teachers in the school to study the history, heritage, and culture of their local community through music, visual arts, and language arts, with a final culminating project presented to both school and community members. This type of investigation, which asks students to think a great deal about the rich musical culture that surrounds their everyday experiences, implicitly values students' musical traditions and builds bridges to their out-of-school experiences.

A teacher and researcher named Dianna Isaac-Johnson (2007) found that her students' motivation to learn increased when she utilized culturally relevant music in her classroom. Isaac-Johnson developed a curriculum for a hip-hop opera in which students watched musical performances, learned songs with the use of a karaoke-type background track, and created new lyrics for these songs. Because the instruction included hip-hop music with which students identified, Isaac-Johnson found her students to be better motivated and more eager to participate.

In addition to utilizing music that relates to students' cultures, teachers can also develop additional performance ensembles such as nontraditional percussion groups, rock ensembles, technology-based ensembles, and mariachi ensembles. Such ensembles do not need to take the place of traditional bands, orchestra, or choirs; as an addition to traditional music offerings, they may resonate with the cultural background of many students who might not otherwise enroll in our traditional music classes and performance ensembles (Boyer-White, 1988; Mixon, 2005).

Culturally Relevant Pedagogy: The Process

Including pieces that represent different cultural traditions in the repertoire of our performance ensembles or general music classes does not, in and of itself, constitute culturally relevant teaching. Our students might or might not enjoy the experience and gain insight into some aspects of certain musical cultures. Multicultural content alone does not automatically lead to increased cultural competency or to better alignment between home and school life for our students. It is the questions we raise and the "teachable moments" we seize, no matter what music we choose, that can provide space for students to be thoughtful about making cultural connections. We must concentrate on the interactions, discussions, questions, dialogue, and explicit and tacit foci of our pedagogy in an attempt to guide students to greater cultural awareness and acceptance (Delpit, 1995; Ladson-Bilings, 1994; Nieto, 2000). It is through our interactions with them that students learn the most about our expectations of them and our intentions in fostering their growth as members of multiple cultural communities.

For example, while teaching high school in Columbus, I combed the archives of my instrumental music library and found a very old score of arranged African American spirituals to sight-read with my high school orchestra. Opening the score, I read in the "notes to the conductor" some antiquated and offensive terminology relating to the African American experience. It was a busy day at the end of the year, and we had much to do, so I wondered whether we should just go ahead and play the piece or whether I should show the passage to my students and open the potentially charged topic for discussion. I chose the latter, and we as a class spent the entire period in an intense discussion of the evolution of racial terminology, the use of certain terms in modern rap songs, and even the use of such terms in our school hallways. I moderated the debate to ensure that all students could have their voices heard. I offered a few probing questions but otherwise let the students debate among themselves. Although we lost almost a full rehearsal that day, my students gained an opportunity to share their opinions as well as the knowledge that their music classroom was a place where difficult and complex discussions of issues such as race were welcome.

Culturally relevant pedagogy asks us as teachers to recognize that it is our primary role to foster an atmosphere where students are encouraged to speak openly, ask questions, and conduct respectful dialogue with each another and with us about relevant issues. To raise these issues alongside the integration of popular, world, or community musics, teachers must be thoughtful about the ways in which they structure their lessons. As Duncan-Andrade and Morrell state (2000), it is extremely important that students are first provided with a "cultural frame" through which they can understand the subject matter being studied. Such a frame provides context for the genre or piece they are learning and encourages a critical examination of the origins of the music, the social structures surrounding musical phenomena, and relevant issues of social justice.

Including popular music in the music classroom opens up opportunities to examine popular culture and how it affects students' lives. Hip-hop provides a very specific example, as many scholars have noted the contradictory nature of hip-hop culture: on one hand, hip-hop has created an Afrocentric focus within the music community that has spurred such social positives as voter registration drives. On the other hand, hip-hop music and music videos often portray violence and the denigration of women (Roach, 2004). As with the example of my orchestra experience in Columbus, the music teacher has the power to create spaces in the classroom where such issues can be raised. When time for thorough discussion of such issues is limited, students can be asked to journal their thoughts about such issues, or even to contribute to a teacher-moderated and password-protected class blog to allow reflection and interaction.

Our pedagogy is reflected, then, not only in our choices for curricular materials but also in how we handle questions, concerns, and dialogue. In this way, even our most informal interactions with students—hallway discussions, end-of-class questions, or mumbled asides—become important parts of our curriculum. Focused on empowering our students, we become cognizant of the many messages that we are sending them with regard to their own cultural identity and the extent to which we embrace different perspectives and viewpoints in our classroom. Our pedagogy becomes culturally relevant when we focus on allowing for meaningful dialogues and interactions to emerge from our music-making.

HIGHLY EFFECTIVE URBAN TEACHERS

When striving to tailor our pedagogy to meet the needs of our students and community, we can gain insight by looking at what sets highly effective teachers of urban students apart from those who may not be as effective. Here, research can help to point out those characteristics, dispositions, and behaviors that are associated with highly effective teachers of urban students. For example, Robinson (2004) interviewed seven master teachers of under-resourced youth from both suburban and urban settings, finding that all of these master teachers stressed the importance of treating each student as an individual with personal strengths, structuring the curriculum to match the diversity of the school population, and purposely seeking to build on student successes. Abril (2006) similarly studied three excellent urban music teachers whose classrooms seemed to stand as "beacons of light" within their schools (p. 79). Through interviews with and observations of each one, Abril found that these teachers were highly attentive and thoughtful educators whose primary goal was to overcome the limitations often imposed by challenges of the urban situation to provide profound musical experiences for their students. Abril noted that a unifying characteristic of all three teachers was their ability to focus on understanding and accommodating the needs of their students.

A researcher named Bussey (2007) investigated the beliefs of successful teachers of African American students and found that these teachers saw themselves as surrogate parents, aunts/uncles, counselors, and friends of their students. These highly successful teachers believed that building a personal relationship with each of their students helped to increase their achievement in school. Kennedy White (2006) found that the teachers in her study who were considered highly successful and culturally competent identified their core beliefs as a commitment to their students, a strong work ethic, high expectations for student work, and the positive belief that all children can be successful. Highly effective teachers of urban students also have a strong sense of self-efficacy (Zhao, 2007), believing strongly in their own capability to meet the demands of teaching at an urban school with competence. Zhao found that this strong sense of self-efficacy is necessary for teachers' persistence and retention within the urban environment (see sidebar, Building Teaching Success).

Martin Haberman, who has studied the attributes of teachers proven to be successful in the urban setting (Haberman, 1993, 2005; Haberman & Post, 1992, 1998), has argued that certain urban teachers are highly

SIDEBAR: BUILDING TEACHING SUCCESS

WHY DO YOU THINK PEOPLE CONSIDER YOU A SUCCESSFUL URBAN MUSIC TEACHER?

Ramon

The number one thing is that you choose to care, and it's all about loving and caring and showing the kids respect. They know if you respect them and you know that they care for you. It's really the secret about teaching; it's love and respect. If they love and respect you, they'll do anything for you. They'll work twice as hard and you're going to work with them as twice as hard. And giving them that loving and caring—that relationship-building—is what makes a good teacher. So I'd like teachers to just be loving, caring, and recognize each student. I'd like them to make sure that the students have an even playing field and to do everything that they can to make sure each student has the best educational environment. That's our job as a teacher, to make sure that they have all the tools necessary to be a success.

Martha

I don't know. I work like crazy. I'm passionate about what I do. To me this is a calling. I think what makes me a good teacher and a successful teacher is that I give 1,000% to whatever I do. That's a priority. I try not to get caught up in the politics because it's just such a pleasure to work with kids. So that's what I try to do. And to speak to the urban side of it—this is something I've become passionate about as a foster parent—school is especially important for kids who are behind the eightball from the start, who have everything going against them, who get thrown into the system and don't have parents to advocate for them or parents who are unable to advocate for them. Oftentimes, school is the only consistent thing in their lives. And to me, you can't change the world, but you can try and change your little corner of it.

Deanna

I work very hard and I get things done and make things happen. I also think it's important to always, when you walk through that door, remember why you're there. It's for the students. That's really important because all of the bureaucratic and system stuff that you go through can wear you down. But if you go in your classroom and close the door and you're with those kids and you make that magic happen, that's what it's about.

Eric

I think people view me as successful because of my students and because of how much my students invest in what we are doing. My students work incredibly hard. They are incredibly caring for each other and for others, and they are warm and supportive and honest with each other. They're able to celebrate their successes and analyze their weaknesses and they're proactive in coming up with solutions to those things. I think my students are the best selling point I have, and I don't say that to be humble. It's just that my students are everything. They are the reason for my success. My presence there has been a catalyst, but it could be any number of two dozen other teachers who could have walked into that building and accomplished the same thing. The most important thing that I've learned about being a teacher is something that I used to think was a cliché and ridiculous. It's that quote that says "People don't care how much you know until they know how much you care." I used to think that, oh, all this psycho-emotional mumbo jumbo is silly. But it's so true. When I show my students love and respect and genuine caring, they respond in spades and they will do anything for me. It's about bringing beauty into their lives and the lives of those around them.

Victoria

The main thing as a music teacher is that you have to inspire children, and you have to do positive things with them. A lot of times, people feel that urban children are different from the suburban students, but I don't think children are much different. I think that some parents ignore their children, whether they're rich or poor. You can't buy a child with money and gifts—you've got to give them attention. You've got to talk with them. You've got to spend time with them.

successful not because they enact certain strategies but that they enact certain successful strategies because they hold compassionate ideologies that "undergird the humane way in which they are able to relate to children and youth" (Haberman, 2005, p. 214). As a result of over 3,000 interviews with teachers, Haberman found that there are important differences between what he calls "star" teachers of children in poverty (according to him, these represent 5% to 8% of all teachers) and teachers who quit or fail within the same schools and school districts. These star teachers are "teachers who, by all common criteria, are outstandingly successful: their students score higher on standardized tests; parents and children think they are great; principals rate them highly; other teachers regard them as outstanding; central office supervisors consider them successful; cooperating universities regard them as superior; and they evaluate themselves as outstanding teachers" (Haberman, 1993, p. 1).

The attributes of highly successful teachers of children in poverty, which Haberman believes cannot be taught in formal educational or teacher education settings, are as follows:

1. They tend to be nonjudgmental. As they interact with children and adults in school settings, their first thought is not to decide the goodness or badness of things, but to understand events in terms of why the children and others do what they do.
2. They are not moralistic. They know that preaching and lecturing is not teaching and does not impact behavior.
3. They respond as professionals and are not easily shocked. Horrific events occur in urban schools with some regularity. They ask themselves, "What can I do about this?" If they think they can do something, they do; otherwise they get on with their work and their lives. They respond to emotionally charged situations as thoughtful professionals.
4. They hear what children and adults say to them. They listen and understand. They have exceedingly sensitive communication skills. They regard listening to everyone in the school community as a potential source of useful information.
5. They recognize and compensate for their weaknesses. They are aware of their own biases and prejudices and strive to overcome them.
6. They do not see themselves as saviors. They have not come to rescue the system. Actually, they do not expect the system to change much,

except to possibly get worse. Their focus is on making their students successful regardless of the system.

7. They are not isolates. They know that burnout can affect everyone. They network and create their own support groups.

8. They view themselves as successful professionals rescuing students. Stars see themselves as "winning" even though they know that their total influence on their students is likely to be less than the total society, the neighborhood, or the gang. They take pride in turning youngsters onto learning and making them educationally successful in the midst of failed urban school systems.

9. They derive energy and well-being from their interactions with children. They enjoy being with children so much that they are willing to put up with even the irrational demands of the system. Rather than always feeling exhausted, there are many days when they feel vitalized and energized from a day at work.

10. They see themselves as teachers of children as well as content. They want their impact on their students to demonstrate that increased learning has made them more humane, better people, not just higher achievers.

11. They are learners. They are models of learning for the children because they are vitally interested in some subject matter or avocation that keeps them constantly learning. They share their love of learning by modeling.

12. They have no need for power. Stars derive great satisfaction from being effective with diverse children in poverty. They are not motivated by any need for power over children, other teachers, or parents.

13. They see the need for diverse children in poverty to succeed in school as a matter of life and death for the students and the survival of society. (Haberman, 2005, pp. 214–215)

This list provides us a glimpse into the types of attributes or characteristics that are shared by those teachers who have been extremely successful in urban schools. It is important to note that just because highly effective teachers tend to share some characteristics does not mean that there are not highly effective urban teachers who differ significantly from the teachers described here. Every teacher is different, and every teacher brings different strengths and weaknesses to the classroom. However, it can be helpful to take a look at others who are successful and learn as much as possible from them.

CONCLUSION

To teach in contextually specific ways is to meet each student where he or she is, recognize the students' prior experiences, and build on their strengths. Throughout this process, a teacher who embraces a contextually specific approach considers and nurtures the identity development of students from all cultural backgrounds. Building a culturally relevant and musically engaging classroom requires a contemplation of curricular and pedagogical strategies as well as an examination of what "works" for those who have found great success as urban teachers. In the next chapter, we will work to apply this understanding to the specialty of music teaching.

CHAPTER 4

Making Music

Having reflected on the needs of our students and strategies for teaching in contextually specific ways, we now need to look at the subject matter we teach—music. This chapter focuses on the process of making and teaching music within the urban music classroom. We begin with a discussion of three domains of music that we may choose to include in our curriculum: the music of the academy, the student, and the community. Then, we explore the specialties of general music, band, orchestra, choir, and mariachi, with specific advice for each provided by Ramon, Martha, Deanna, Eric, and Victoria.

WHOSE MUSIC DO I TEACH?

In any music teaching setting, we are likely to select music and music-making activities that have meant the most to us in our own experience. Sometimes the music that we value and cherish will be valued and cherished by our students. Sometimes it will not, and for the most part, this is an acceptable situation. One important aspect of any type of education is exposure to experiences outside a student's own preferences and knowledge. However, if the music and musical activities that we choose to utilize within our classroom are so far removed from the experiences and understandings of our students that they cannot see any connection whatsoever to their lives, their level of motivation to learn the material as well as their comprehension of it will undoubtedly be reduced.

In the field of music education, it is sometimes difficult for us as teachers to think in new and innovative ways about the music and musical activities that we choose for our classes. Our profession does not change quickly; there are generally certain compositions and ways of learning them that have been ingrained in each of us as being "essential" due to the time we have spent in music education programs as students ourselves. For example, when I began my career teaching high school band, I approached the selection of music for my first adjudicated concert band festival as do many beginning music teachers: I chose a program of music that I myself had played and enjoyed during my time as a high school trumpet player. I soon realized that the strengths and weaknesses of my current ensemble were very different from those of the ensemble I had played with when I was a high school student. I had to acknowledge that the music I had chosen was not the most appropriate for the needs and strengths of my students. Over the years, I learned how to select music and music-making experiences for my students that were better tailored to their unique needs and that built on the knowledge they already had. However, during that first year, my own experience was my security, and I clung to it! When we decide to take the needs, preferences, experiences, and motivations of our students into account in selecting music and music-making activities, we are teaching in ways that engage our students in relevant and positive learning experiences. Next, I present three broad categories of music from which educators typically select repertoire: music of the academy, music of the student, and music of the community. I argue that regardless of where they place the most emphasis, music teachers should engage students with music from each of these three domains at some point each year.

As music teachers who have been highly educated as performing musicians within institutions of higher education, we are generally most familiar with the music of the academy, otherwise known as Western art music. It is predominant in our experiences as students because most higher education music programs accept only applicants who can already perform Western art music at a high level; anyone accomplished in other musical traditions is generally not welcomed into programs of music teacher education in the United States (Fitzpatrick, Henninger, & Taylor, 2014). Western art music is made up of a canon of compositions that have lasted through the ages and have become meaningful to many people. Below, music philosopher Estelle Jorgensen (2003) provides a rationale for why it may be important to study Western art music:

> The term "Western classical music" is a misnomer. It is really a multi-cultural and international tradition forged by musicians around the world who brought their various individual and cultural perspectives to a music that grew up in Europe but that from its infancy drew upon African and Near Eastern roots. Its widespread influence as one of the great musical traditions does not make it necessarily better than others, but does make it worthy of study. A music that is known so widely, has captured the interest and participation of so many musicians and their audiences internationally, has such a rich repertory, and represents so many cultures strikes me as a human endeavor of inherent interest and worth. (p. 134)

Many of our students may find Western art music intimidating because of the complex structure and length of typical "classical" compositions. It is important, therefore, that we help them develop some sort of literacy with this domain, lest they be permanently excluded from participating in its richness.

In deciding how much of a role the "music of the academy" should play within our classroom, we should consider the needs of our students balanced against all the other rich domains of music that could be included in our curriculum. When we do introduce students to "classical" music, whether within general music classes or performing ensembles, there are many ways that we can help to make it relevant to and exciting for them. Eric talks about how he introduces classical music to his students:

> As beginners, they're definitely resistant to it. But I think that, like with anything else, the more they learn about it, the more they appreciate it. The thing that I always do that sucks them in is I find just two pieces of music. First, I try to find one that is just stunningly beautiful and gorgeous that my students can really sort of soak in and absorb and feel and sense that beauty in themselves.

Then, I try to find something upbeat and dynamic and vibrant and big and loud and rhythmic. Once they hear these extreme examples, they say that, oh, classical music isn't all boring—it isn't all completely uninteresting. They're captivated by some of these carefully selected examples that pique their interest. After that, they're kind of hooked, and I challenge them to go explore on their own. So students are routinely bringing me suggestions for music that we should sing, and saying, oh, I heard this on You Tube (which is so helpful for this type of thing), or, I heard this beautiful song that some choir did—I really want to do it. I try to pique their interest enough that they'll explore it themselves, because I can spit information at them all day and they won't care. I've got to stir up something inside of them, and then they love it. They just can't get enough.

Music of Our Students

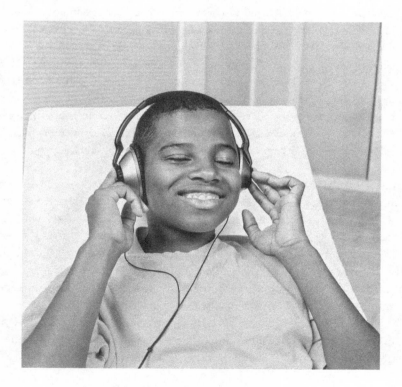

As teachers, we are often less familiar with the music of our students—or the music that our students appreciate and cherish as an everyday part of their lives. Most often, this is popular music. Although some of us may appreciate certain types of popular music, we may not know the music our

SIDEBAR: TEACHING WITH POPULAR MUSIC

SHARING STRATEGIES THAT WORK

Ramon

A lot of times, I tell the students to bring in specific songs, albums, or playlists so they can tell us what songs they like, and what they would like to hear. What we do is we use some of that music and arrange it for the mariachi ensemble. Mariachi music is like Christmas music. It's music that their grandma knows, their grandfather knows, everybody knows, and it makes it part of the family. So what they really like is that they get to be part of the student-led learning, where it's not the teacher telling them this is the song that you need to play. I really enjoy that, and the students really enjoy that, too, because they work even harder when they get to be part of the decision-making process.

Martha

I try to find popular songs that have samples of classical pieces in them. For example, I was teaching about Beethoven's Fifth and "Fur Elise," and then I played them a song by the rap singer Nas called "I Can" that has a sample of "Fur Elise" in the background. It's this rap song that samples Beethoven. I'd play "Fur Elise" on the piano. And they all know that melody and they all like that melody, and then we put it on with the rap song and then they really loved it. And this coming year, I'm starting a rock ensemble for the kids that I learned about through a professional development day. Basically their idea is that most rock songs only have two or three chords. So you start with that, and you get the whole class jamming on one or two chords while you have this other set of kids play a simple bass line and this other set of kids do a simple percussion part. And it sounded amazing. I'm looking forward to doing that with my kids.

Deanna

We have a popular music concert in the spring. In the beginning of the year, we're working on technique and we're working on all the classical things that we need to do for festivals and such, but I lose some kids at that time. So I bring it all back in the spring. Around April, I tell the students that they need to get me what music they'd like me to orchestrate, and there are certain rules about language and things like that. It's on them to kind of pick out the pieces, and then we discuss what will work for strings and what really won't work for strings. And we put percussion to it. They're great concerts, and they really enjoy that part. I mean, that kind of brings back those kids that were not having great success at the reading and then I can keep them for another year and we can go through that again. Some years it's good and some years it's not as good.

And some kids are not as drawn to that as they are hooked on some of the other repertoire that we've done like Vivaldi or something.

Eric

I didn't use it for a long time. I refused. I said, I'm going to teach classical music. And I used to sing pop music for a living, so that was a little different for me. But I always felt like the pop music that is out there that is published is just crap, and didn't want to cheapen their experience. So I have always done solely classical music, and to be honest, my students ate it up. They couldn't get enough. They loved it. And it's only actually recently that I started incorporating popular music into my curricula. We now do a pop song or two, and it initially started as an extracurricular activity, where we did a little studio recording project. We spent a couple hundred bucks on some gear and recorded in the pop a capella style just for kicks—just for fun. Now, the students are just eating it up and they want to do it in class. It doesn't matter to them that the song is 30 years old—they don't care. Stylistically, we made it relevant to them, and the lyrics are still relevant too. I think they appreciate the diversity in the styles and the different skills that are needed to perform pop music. I push hard on my students to learn independent musicianship skills, including reading and sight-reading and playing piano. But the rote skills that are so handy for pop music are also something that's really valuable. So it's been a really good opportunity to teach them those skills and how those skills are different and how they reinforce each other. They're not exclusive. And neither of them is better than the other.

Victoria

At the beginning of the school year, I usually do some popular music because that captures the students right away. If I want to teach the kids how to count rhythms, I'll take rhythms out of the popular songs and I'll make up rhythm sheets. They like popular music, and the popular music has very difficult rhythms in it. It's a good way to capture them for the fall and to entice other children to join. So I do it at the beginning of the year. We also arrange a lot of popular songs for my band to play. I have a group of alumni from my school who can write anything that I need. I can tell them to listen to it, and they can arrange it for my band.

students listen to or how to utilize it in our classrooms. Deciding if and how to include some of it in our curriculum requires investigation on our part.

As an urban music teacher, I recall hearing my students break out into small, informal rap groups in the hallways between classes. I would listen to them rapping with one another in these small groups and wonder how I, as their music teacher, had such little understanding of this music that they obviously enjoyed making. It was almost completely improvise seemed to require a sophisticated understanding of both rhythmi melodic conventions. It also used a lot of language that was inappi ate for the school (which is why students generally used hushed tones in the hallways), which presented another problem for me in figuring out how I could work with this music in my classroom. Our panel of successful urban music teachers, however, has some ideas for incorporating popular music into the music classroom; several of these are included in the following sidebar, Teaching with Popular Music.

An obvious advantage to using popular music in the classroom is that students will likely bring tremendous motivation to discuss, experience, and learn about music that they enjoy. One of the greatest advantages of the technological revolution is the increased access to music it has brought across our society. For a relatively small expenditure, our students can carry with them a small device that can access thousands of pieces of music. As music teachers, we should delight in this improved accessibility of music to students from across the socioeconomic spectrum. However, they still need to understand this music that they listen to, and it would be even better if we could teach them to compose and play it themselves! This is where we come in as music teachers—whether our students listen to rap, rock, hip-hop, reggaeton, country, punk, metal, merengue, pop, or any other genre of music that they claim as their own, we as music teachers can help them understand, appreciate, perform, arrange, compose, and improvise popular music.

Music of the Community

The third domain of music to consider within our curriculum is the music of our students' community—both local and global. By the local community, I refer to the rich musical traditions embraced by the communities, neighborhoods, and cultural institutions that surround the places where our students live. By the global community, I refer to music of the different cultures and nations of the world, many of which are already familiar to our students because of their own cultural background and heritage. Many of these local and global music traditions, such as the mariachi music that Ramon has been so successful in incorporating into his music program, relate to our students' ethnic or racial identity. Some of these types of music come from religious traditions that are important to certain populations who live in our communities, and still others are based on folk music traditions that relate to the geographic location in which our students live. For example, musical traditions that may be important to our students' communities include gospel music of the Black church, klezmer music, polka music, mariachi, bluegrass, zydeco, and Appalachian folk music, among others.

If you teach in a school where a strong musical tradition is embraced by the surrounding community, you have a terrific advantage. Although you may not know this music yourself, you can find ways to bring it into your music classroom in authentic ways—see the sidebar, Performing Multicultural Music, for tips on how to do this well. Many parents of your students (or even students themselves) would be delighted to come and work with your classes to share a part of their culture. Learning such music also enables you to consider designing exciting new performance opportunities for your students, such as community concerts in a local park, cultural heritage programs, or partnership concerts with local performing groups. By building bridges with the local community in these ways, you may find a richness of musical experience that greatly enhances your students' learning as well as your own.

For example, Martha and Eric have found various ways to incorporate the music of their community into their classrooms. Martha tells how she tailors the music that she teaches to the background of the students enrolled in her general music classes:

> I surveyed the kids about their ethnic backgrounds, and then I gathered all that data and determined the biggest groups. And then we would first take the ethnicity that was most represented among the students, which I think was probably students with Dominican heritage. And so I did a unit on the music of the Dominican Republic. I did a lot of talking with those students to learn about their country and their background and their families as well as studying the music myself, because I didn't know a lot of these countries, and I had no idea what the music from those countries was. So that was how I approached it in the beginning. Then, I went down by percentage to the next group that was most represented, say Puerto Rican, then we studied the music of Puerto Rico and so forth.

Eric also includes music from his students' culture in his choir's repertoire. He discusses here how he approaches learning music that may be unfamiliar to him:

> I incorporate a huge degree of multicultural music in our repertoire and we typically sing in 10 or 12 different languages over the course of the year. The obvious examples are when there are schoolwide assemblies for the Chinese New Year,

SIDEBAR: STRATEGIES FOR PERFORMING MULTICULTURAL MUSIC WITH AUTHENTICITY

If you would like to have your students and ensembles perform pieces of music from various cultures, Mary Goetze provides some terrific suggestions for ways to make the musical experience as authentic as possible:

1. Honor the culture by deferring to the experts: native musicians from that culture. You can either speak with them in person or ask permission to make a video or audio recording of them.
2. Speak with a native artist or cultural representative to determine the appropriateness of the ensemble learning the music and performing it for others.
3. Learn as much as you can about the culture from written and video resources, and share the information with your students.
4. If possible, invite a native of the culture to meet the ensemble, either in person or virtually, in order to foster a personal connection with the group.
5. Have the ensemble learn the music aurally—especially if it is transmitted that way within the culture. If using a score, have the students first learn the piece aurally, and then have them compare what they heard and learned to what is and is not symbolized in the printed music.
6. In leading students to explore unfamiliar methods of vocal production, educate them about their voices, but be sensitive to individual limitations.
7. Have the students imitate the visual aspects of the performance carefully, especially any movement, as, in many cultures, dance, dress, and even context and community are inseparable from sound.
8. For vocal pieces, record a native performer who can pronounce and translate the text.
9. Show your respect for the culture by re-creating the music with integrity—match your performance as nearly as possible to the model.
10. Explore performing music without a conductor, if appropriate to the tradition
11. Share information about the music and culture with the audience through program notes, or, if possible, spoken comments by the native performer.

(Adapted from Goetze, 2000, p. 25)

or for Cinco de Mayo, or African American heritage club. We will, for example, learn a traditional Chinese song in Mandarin or Cantonese and perform that as part of those celebrations. To learn them, I just ask my students. I say, hey look, we're going to sing a song for the Chinese New Year, and my Chinese students just bombard me with suggestions. And I sit down with a couple of my student advisors and we sort through the songs and figure out which ones we want to do because they always have favorites. So we do that for our Mexican, Chinese, and African American populations. For my students, it's something that's just sort of routine, and they see it as a way to support their community, to support each other, and to support the diversity within the school. They really believe in it as a way to reach out to each other and make our school a stronger place. So, the students are a tremendous resource. I've tried to engage parents, but that's been a real struggle. There is also a local Mexican band that focuses on traditional music of Mexico that has been helpful. Reaching out to artists in the community can be very valuable.

These three domains of music—that of the academy, that of the student, and that of the community—provide us with a tremendous diversity of musical traditions from which we can choose to best address the educational needs of our students. They are certainly not the only possible musical domains. For example, one could also add ensemble-specific musical traditions (such as brass band music, barbershop music, etc.). However, the three I've concentrated on are important to consider when making judgments about the types of music and musical experiences to include in our classrooms.

We, as music teachers, often have a good deal of leeway in what kinds of music to incorporate within our curriculum based on our knowledge of the context in which we teach and our best judgment as to the experiences that will most benefit our students and their musical understanding. These different domains of music have been described here to encourage you to be thoughtful of the many ways that one can be musical, and to inspire you to consider the musical traditions that surround you and your students.

CONSIDERING OUR TEACHING SPECIALTIES

Although this book addresses the urban music teaching context in general, I would be remiss if I did not allow some time to reflect on the particularities of the music specialties that each of us may find ourselves teaching at different times. To address the specifics of teaching mariachi, general music, strings, choir, or band in urban settings, I have asked each of the panel teachers to offer brief words of advice that speak specifically to urban music teachers of their specialty. In the following section, you will find their brief thoughts on urban teaching within each of these specialties.

Mariachi: Ramon

I think that we should encourage people to use any kind of multicultural music that they can in their curriculum. I love classical music, and I think classical music is great, but there's so much music out there, even with

mariachi music. You could study and study about music and you'll still only know about 5% of the music that is out there in the world. I think mariachi is a great way to diversify your program. If you want to start a mariachi program, there are a lot of resources. There's the National Mariachi Educators Association—they have a big conference in Las Vegas where they teach band and choir and orchestra teachers how to teach mariachi in their schools. You have to have, one, a love for kids and, two, a love for music. You need to be able to read a score and teach the basic instruments of mariachi, which are guitar, violin, and trumpet. As a music teacher, you should be able to teach trumpet and violin and guitar, so it's not so different. In band, you have to learn to play 20 different instruments, and in mariachi there are only five total, so I think you could include this in your curriculum, especially if you have a Hispanic population. The language might be a barrier, but Hal Leonard, one of the biggest music publishers out there, has a mariachi series with CDs and scores and a guide. I think that with the students helping to lead and also getting some help in starting, it can be done. If you can read a score, you can teach mariachi.

General Music: Martha

I have to say that general music is where my heart is, and I think one of the great things about general music is the teacher's ability to tie it into other things that are happening in the school. I've always sort of thought that the great thing about being the music teacher is that any subject can be tied into what we're doing, and a lot of times we're putting on shows and doing things where you can really collaborate with other people and really talk to the whole school community. As the general music teacher, you have a voice that helps the whole school set a certain sort of tone. For example, when I talk about doing multicultural projects and different themed units, I think it's a way to get your colleagues excited about an idea. And it just makes it more fun for all of us to be there.

Strings: Deanna

I would go right to technique if you're a string teacher. Make sure you start away from the book and make sure technique is there, just as you would in any other school. It's an instrument and any kid is going to be thrilled to play an instrument, right? I have a whole rap that I do at the beginning of the fourth grade class, and I made it up a while back. In the rap, we learn all of the safety things about the instruments, and how there's horse hair on the bow, and if the bridge falls down, Ms. Martinez will put it up. I can see any kid in my school, or any kid on the street that was in my class years ago, and I could do the rap with him. I mean, a whole auditorium, I could get going. It's fun.

Choir: Eric

Repertoire is huge. It doesn't matter to me if it's classical or popular styles, if you're not choosing really, truly compelling, exceptional repertoire, you won't stand a chance. And I think that's a huge challenge for new teachers, because they've never done it before. It was a huge challenge for me. I didn't know what to do. I mean, I've been singing choral music since I was 10, so I had some staples that I fell back on, and thank goodness they worked. I think choosing music that is within the range of your students' immediate abilities is important. I see teachers routinely choose music that is well beyond the ability of their students. An eight-part spiritual for a beginning chorus is just not going to happen with certain groups.

I think the other thing for me is that so much of choral music is about who we are as human beings, and about how we feel about ourselves, and about how we feel about our own voice, not just our physical singing voice, but our voice as a student, our voice as a young man or woman. I think that tying their choral singing voice to their voice as a human being to their voice as a student and as a young man or as a young woman is really important and really valuable, because so many of these students don't have a voice. They don't have a voice at home, they don't have a voice at school, they don't have a voice at work. To tie those things together, I tell my students all the time that you have to find your voice, and that the progress that they make with their singing voice can mirror the process that they make with their human voice. I think that's an incredibly important way to make choral music valuable to them, because they see those parallels too. I think that tying choral music into their basic humanity is the most important thing of all that we can do.

Band: Victoria

As a band teacher in an urban school like mine, you may find yourself teaching beginners at the high school level, rather than working with students who've already studied their instrument in elementary or middle school. Because they are beginners and because we have a lot of mobility, it feels like you start all over every year. They have great musical instincts, but you can't assume that anybody knows a lot of the formal musical elements like reading music or being able to count rhythms unless you've been working with them—it is just too rare that they have had experience in band prior to high school. Every year, you are teaching the basic things. Sometimes you can move a little faster than others. So, at the beginning it's about teaching the clapping and counting and making sure they're writing the beats in, making sure that they know the letter names of the notes. I found that in order to capture the students and help them past this phase, they need to play. They need to perform, and that's so important when they're starting out. Even at the beginning of the year, they need to start out with songs not that they played before but something new so that everybody has a challenge of having to learn something. Every year I have to do that, at the beginning of every year. We have to keep encouraging our students and being positive as we start over each year.

Also, the marching band, that gets you your recognition. That's when people know about you. You can have the best band in the world sitting in that school, but a lot of times when you call people to see if they want a band to perform, they don't want a concert band. They want somebody who can come right in and get right out, and a marching band can move right in. We can play all types of music. We can play marches. We play a lot of popular stuff, but we play things that people recognize, so people will recognize a marching band, and marching bands can go anywhere.

CHAPTER 5

Rejecting the "One Size Fits All" Model

Setting Your Own Definition of Music Program Success

As urban music teachers, we often fulfill many roles: educator, conductor, performer, counselor, psychologist, fundraiser . . . even custodian! We often are so busy with the different aspects of our job that we don't have time to reflect on our goals for our program and reevaluate whether the experiences we are providing align with the needs of our students, school, and community. Although some of our curricular content is pre-determined by district or state curricular standards, we usually have some degree of flexibility. For example, we usually choose what music we believe best meets the needs of our students and decide what format our concerts and performances will take. Most music teachers also make important decisions regarding their students' participation in festivals/contests, schoolwide interdisciplinary projects, elective courses, performance trips, extra concerts, and recording projects. In sum, we make many pedagogical decisions that influence the types of experiences our students will have within our music program, and these decisions become part of the curriculum that our students experience.

Contemplating curricular change is a healthy process for any self-reflective teacher, and should happen in all settings—urban, suburban, and rural. However, one of the foundational premises of this book is that great teaching should be contextually specific, or, tailored to meet the individualized needs of each school and student. To do this, we must be open to continual re-assessment of and invigoration of our music program's goals, according to the evolving strengths of our students. Within this chapter, I ask you to spend some time contemplating the overarching goals that you have for your music program, as well as the musical experiences you plan for your students. I ask you to carefully reevaluate and reprioritize these goals and experiences according to the current needs of your program, students, and community. Through this process, I hope that you will discover creative and innovative ideas for maximizing the learning experiences of your students.

WHAT DOES SUCCESS MEAN TO YOU?

Music teachers in all settings try to plan musical experiences and set goals for their programs that they feel are in the best interests of their students. However, often our goals for our program are derived from how we have traditionally defined success. Our definitions of success frequently come from our own experiences—we often carry on the same traditions that we experienced (or wish that we had experienced) as students ourselves. Try to think about how you define a "successful music program." For most American band, choir, and orchestra programs, many would agree that success has traditionally been defined as the achievement of goals related to such things as high ratings at festivals and contests, a large number of students enrolled in the music program, a visible presence in the community, the performance of challenging pieces of music from the standard canon, and a number of students who may go on to choose music as a college major, among others. For general music teachers, success for their program may be defined in similar ways, but also include such other things as the presentation of highly coordinated schoolwide concerts/assemblies, interdisciplinary collaborations with other teachers within the school, and the development of co- or extra-curricular specialized ensembles.

Many of these are certainly noble aims for our music programs and could possibly lead our students to a deep and profound experience with music. For that reason, many of us will, through the process of goal-setting described in this chapter, choose some of these experiences as being of continued importance to meet our students' needs. However, we also may feel, upon reflection, that some of these musical experiences do not align well with the needs/strengths of our students, nor the resources available to us. We may need to set a new definition of success for our music program that centers around the aim of developing our particular students' long-term understanding of, appreciation for, and love of music. We then may decide to maintain a few of these traditional musical experiences, lose a few, and strategically add a few others that may better align with the current needs of our students and the resources available to us. Others of us may choose to completely transform the types of experiences that we are providing to our students. I encourage you to consider that success in any particular setting must be defined according to what will best meet the needs of the students in that particular school. We need to try to let go of our own predetermined definitions of music program success and redefine what success means to our students and program.

Here, I propose, is where our understanding of our students and community (which we have discussed in the previous chapters) begins to align with our pedagogical and curricular knowledge. We must work to design and develop meaningful learning opportunities for our students that are tailored to their needs, not to the needs of the students who go to school in the next town, and not to the school that we ourselves attended. There should be no "one size fits all" music program that we "implement" across every setting. To be most effective, the goals and musical experiences that you plan for your music program must be tailored to meet the unique needs of your students, your school, and your community.

In the pages that follow, I ask you to carefully reflect upon the curriculum that is currently in place for your students. I ask you to consider the goals you might want to establish for your program and to reexamine how your existing curriculum aligns with those goals. Throughout this process, the primary considerations that should guide your thinking are the particular needs, strengths, and prior knowledge that your students bring to the classroom. As discussed in the previous chapters, this is your primary resource as well as your primary responsibility. However, there are some other factors that can and should influence the goals that we set for our program and the musical experiences that we plan; these are described next.

PLANNING MUSICAL EXPERIENCES: INFLUENCES ON OUR GOAL-SETTING

As we work on setting goals and planning musical experiences that are uniquely tailored to address our students' needs, there are many issues that we need to consider. For example, if, within my elementary general music program, I have a group of advanced students who are in need of an extra challenge, I could plan to establish a new after-school elective Orff Ensemble at my school. However, if my administration doesn't allow extended access to the building after school, if many of the parents of my students work multiple jobs and thus cannot arrange transportation home from such an activity, and if my students are more interested in the after-school soccer league than my Orff Ensemble, then I have not set myself, my students, or my program up for success by diverting resources to this new opportunity. In setting goals and planning musical experiences based upon the needs of our students, we must be mindful of the following:

1. The expectations of stakeholders such as administrators, parents, and community members, based in part on the history/tradition of our music programs;
2. The resources available to us to facilitate our plans; and
3. The degree to which we are able to motivate our students to be successful with the activities and goals that we have planned.

The Expectations of Stakeholders

To set goals that allow for student success, it is important that you consider the expectations of stakeholders who care deeply about your students and your music program. If you were the only one with a vested interest in your program and students, you could make the changes that you felt were in the best interests of your students without consulting others. However, most music programs are of sufficient visibility in their schools and communities that a number of stakeholders contribute to a set of expectations for what your music program might "do." You may, for example, wish to eliminate a keyboard class that has been taught for years because you feel that your students who enroll have no real interest in learning how to play the keyboard, and you can envision other classes or activities that might be more relevant to them. However, you may have administrators who greatly prize the keyboard classes that you teach because such a program serves a large number of students and presents a wonderful alternative to a study hall that they would otherwise have to create. Obviously, you cannot just decide to eliminate the large keyboard class and teach a smaller "history of rock" course without gaining the support of your administrators.

Similarly, although you personally may feel that a highly competitive marching band program is not in the best interests of your particular students, you may need to acknowledge that your school and the band program have a strong tradition with regard to competition, and that the parents and community members take great pride in the marching band's success at competitions. Simply deciding to do away with the competitive aspects of your program without the support of these important stakeholders would be detrimental to your career as well as to the future of any innovative ideas that you might be able to offer students within your program. Thus, you must consider the expectations of the school and the larger community before planning changes.

What are the expectations and values of important stakeholders at your school? Take a moment to complete Table 5.1, Expectations and Values of Music Program Stakeholders. What aspects of your current program are most valued by each of these populations? Outlining the expectations and values that they appear to hold most dear may help you decide how to prioritize the changes that you feel are most important to make.

As you list the expectations of these different individuals and groups, try to think critically about how they align with the needs of your students. If you agree that they align well with what you see as your students' particular needs and strengths, then your path forward to setting goals and outlining musical experiences should be rather smooth. You can feel confident that your ideas will be supported within your school community, and that your music program will be embraced by those stakeholders who can assist your goals for growth and revitalization.

Deciding what to do when your goals clash with those of important stakeholders depends on the type of influence or human capital you have with

Table 5.1. EXPECTATIONS AND VALUES OF MUSIC PROGRAM STAKEHOLDERS

Stakeholders	What are the top 3 things that this stakeholder most values as a part of your music program?
Administrators (e.g., high ratings at festival, large student enrollment, engagement with other teachers)	1. 2. 3.
Parents (e.g., several high-profile assemblies, an annual musical, positive student social interactions)	1. 2. 3.
Community Members (e.g., participation in local parades, occasional performances at local nursing homes)	1. 2. 3.
Students (e.g., biannual trips, performing popular music occasionally)	1. 2. 3.

those particular people. If you are in your first or second year at your school, if you are an inexperienced teacher, or if you are concerned about whether you have built sufficient confidence and trust with students, parents, administrators, or community members, you may need to go along with what exists for a time until you build sufficient influence with those stakeholders and can start making incremental changes. In the meantime, you may wish to "add" new ideas, concerts, activities, and programs rather than "taking away" or changing anything about your program that seems important to those stakeholders. Eventually, as you establish greater trust and respect, you will be able to begin holding conversations about your long-term goals for your program. Change will come—it just may take a while.

If, however, you disagree with some of the expectations that others have for your program, and you have sufficient influence, experience, trust, and confidence established with them, you may be able to initiate your ideas for change or revitalization right away. When you do so, it is important that you give sufficient notice of your plans for change, explain in detail your plans for the initiation of new ideas or replacement of old ones, and try in advance to find certain stakeholders who will support you through the process (the well-respected kindergarten teacher down the hall? Your booster president?

The school counselor? Your choir officers?). During periods of change or revitalization, if you are thoughtful about how you manage relationships with important stakeholders, you will be more likely to achieve success.

Taking Inventory: Examining Your Resources

We, and our students, cannot be successful if we do not have the necessary resources to achieve our goals. It's a terrific idea, for example, to begin a "strolling strings" program at your middle school, but without enough school-owned instruments for kids who need them, you obviously can't involve enough students to achieve your goal. It's also exciting to think about collaborating with the classroom teachers at your elementary school on a schoolwide musical, but without sufficient collaborative planning time, you are unlikely to have success. It is important that you identify the resources that you currently have in place before you plan for the future, and work to identify new resources that may be necessary to achieve your goals.

When I speak of resources, I do not mean only financial resources. These are important, but there are many other kinds of resources to consider with regard to your music program. For example, each of the following is a type of resource that is important to the success of any music program. Carefully consider which of these resources you are in need of and which you have in abundance:

- Financial funding
- Available personnel/staff
- Music-making materials (instruments of all kinds, sheet music, recordings, etc.)
- Administrative materials (access to copiers, e-mail, phone, social media, student/parent contact information, etc.)
- External music enrichment for students (students taking private lessons, students enrolled in honor groups, children's choirs, etc.)
- Supportive atmosphere that enables creativity/risk-taking (in your classroom, in your school)
- Access to technology
- Time to schedule classes/rehearsals/performances (student/parent availability after school, flexibility of school class schedule, sufficient contact time with students)
- Space to schedule classes/rehearsals/performances
- Adequacy of transportation (after school, to performances/trips)
- Your own time and excitement

- Administrative and collegial support (a positive "tone" or atmosphere regarding the program)
- Student investment and motivation to succeed (more information on this in the next section)
- Cultural richness or diversity of students (the background and experiences of students, leading to a diversity of ideas, approaches, and insights that can enrich the classroom)
- Consistent student participation (lack of student mobility and/or ways to resolve scheduling conflicts)
- Tradition of excellence upon which to build (in terms of both musical caliber of the program and excitement about the music program's place in the school culture)
- Helpful or supportive parent/alumni base
- Sufficient student retention (good recruiting, feeder programs, etc.)
- Community arts resources (helpful area arts organizations, private lesson teachers, professional musical organizations)

The first step to aligning our goals with our resources is to find out what we currently have. Similar to reconciling a checkbook, we first need to take inventory of what is in our "account" of resources. As you go through the previous list, be very, very honest about "what is"—this is a time to identify what is present and what is lacking. Do not be overwhelmed if you have very little currently available; we cannot move forward unless we know what we already have.

Don't forget to take stock of the final category: community arts resources. Although many people often discuss the challenges of teaching in an urban environment, they often neglect the unique resources that exist in urban communities. Often, living and teaching in an urban community means that you probably have some sort of arts organization or ensemble nearby—a symphony, military field band, opera company, professional chorus, theater, college or university music department, museum, or other arts resources. These organizations offer tremendous opportunities for collaboration, whether in the form of short-term field trips or residencies, or longer-term partnerships with your students and music program. As you take stock of your resources, it's a good idea to make contact with them and see what they can offer. For example, Deanna talks about the resources she has found in Detroit and how she capitalizes on them to enhance her students' learning:

We're really fortunate with where the school is located. For the past two years, the Detroit Symphony Orchestra (DSO) has come to our school to do a performance for the whole school. Sometimes I make the phone call at the right time. After they performed for us the first year, I called the DSO and said, hey, if you don't have a school picked out yet to perform at, we're right in your neighborhood. Why don't you come on back? And they did it. And it was just amazing. And then we have the Scarab Club Chamber players near us as well. On Friday mornings we can walk to the Scarab Club and hear some French impressionist music, chamber music, and see art. There are other ones as well—the Chamber Music Society of Detroit comes to our school, and we had the American String Quartet most recently—they played the Ravel quartet. It's really been great to have that sort of connectedness with local arts organizations. My advice—reach out to the people in charge of the education departments, and say, we're interested.

Once you have taken inventory of what you currently have, you need to carefully evaluate what you'd like to do and what you'd like to plan, given these resources. When we are faced with a lack of resources to achieve our goals, we have two options: we can either find a way to get the needed resources (ask for donations, write a grant, build a relationship with the school scheduling person, start a booster group, etc.) or we need to redefine our goals to better align with the resources we do have (start a music technology class because we have wonderful technological resources available, develop a hip-hop unit because students are highly motivated with regard to popular music, put on a student-written opera in collaboration with the wonderfully supportive drama teacher and an industrial technology teacher who builds terrific sets, etc.). That's why it is so important for us to take inventory before we set our goals.

My students were always motivated by going to district concert band festival. They loved it, and my community, parents, and administration expected that we would go each year in a very challenging grade level category (Class A in Ohio). However, I only had two to three students taking private lessons in any given year. This put us at a distinct disadvantage when compared with the other groups who would play alongside us at our judged festivals. We did not have the needed resources available to us, so if I wanted to achieve success and promote a culture of excellence within my program, I needed to either find a way to get students individualized attention on their instruments or re-evaluate whether going to festival was a great goal for us. I chose to continue going to festival (again, because my students enjoyed it, it was motivating for them, and my stakeholders most certainly expected it), but recognized that I needed to structure things in a different way.

I arranged after-school sectional rehearsals so that I could teach instrument-specific skills, brought in friends who would work with my students for no charge, spent a great deal of time within rehearsals on instrument-specific concepts, and held weekend retreats where students came to work with local clinicians (they donated their services) who helped them improve. This is how we were able to achieve success—because we recognized what we had and didn't have, and gathered the resources necessary to succeed. It's also all right to let go of traditional activities for which we don't have sufficient resources, and substitute others that will better suit the needs of our students and our program. But these are our only options: we either need to find a way to get the needed resources to promote excellence at what we're trying to do, or we need to redefine our goals so that they better align with the resources that we do have. In order to cultivate a culture of excellence, whatever we do, we need to do it well—this is how momentum is achieved, and this is how great music programs are built, even when they have few financial resources.

ESTABLISHING NEW GOALS AND EXPERIENCES

Now that you have considered the expectations of important stakeholders and have seen what resources you have available to you at this moment, it's time to plan and to dream. To start the process of re-examining your program goals and better poising yourself and your students for success, take a look at Table 5.2, Envisioning Your Goals. Keeping in mind the particular needs and strengths of your students, and thinking of the longer term (the next five years), what types of goals do you feel are most important? Use your best judgment here—if you have carefully considered the needs of your students and have worked hard to get to know them, then you are likely in a good position to set these goals. Try to set goals that will take your students' needs into account, be supported by important stakeholders, and align well with existing or potential resources. You will notice that I ask you to consider different kinds of goals: for your students' musical growth, for their personal growth, for you as a music teacher, and for your program overall. I do this to help you see the interconnected nature of all of these aspects that are so important to your program's success and thus the success of your students.

Once you've outlined the goals that you feel are most important for your program, take a look at Table 5.3, Program Profile. It lets you take a close look at your current program in light of your new goals. In the first column, list all of the major musical experiences and processes that you planned for

Table 5.2. ENVISIONING YOUR GOALS

Envisioning Your Goals
LOOKING AHEAD TO THE NEXT FIVE YEARS, AND TAKING INTO ACCOUNT THE PARTICULAR NEEDS OF YOUR STUDENTS, CONSIDER THE GOALS THAT YOU WOULD LIKE TO SET WITH REGARD TO THE FOLLOWING DOMAINS:
Top Goals for your Students: Musical Experiences (e.g., I want every one of my students to have the opportunity to play culturally diverse music; I want every student to feel comfortable improvising) M1. M2. M3.
Top Goals for Your Students: Personal Growth (e.g., I want my students to have the opportunity to develop their leadership skills; I want my students to become more supportive of their own and one another's mistakes) S1. S2. S3.
Top Goals for You as a Teacher: (e.g., I want to attend my state's music education or multicultural education conference every year in order to gather ideas and network with other teachers; I want to establish a more positive classroom culture through developing my classroom management skills) T1. T2. T3.
Top Goals for Your Music Program: (e.g., I want this program to increase the number of students participating; I want to increase the amount of pride that students have in the program) P1. P2. P3.

this past year. Don't include state or district mandated curricula that you have no freedom to change; include only those concerts, performances, and procedures that you as a teacher are responsible for imagining, planning, and executing.

In the second column, thoughtfully and honestly consider the degree to which you and your students are able to achieve "excellence" with and through that particular musical experience. By "excellence," I mean that to really meet the needs of our students, and invigorate our program, we must make sure that when we do things, we do them well. Doing things half-heartedly or

Table 5.3. PROGRAM PROFILE			
Musical Experiences	Honest Assessment	Alignment with Goals	Keep, Revise, or Toss
List here major musical activities for your program, such as concerts, trips, performances, daily routines, etc.	On a scale from 1–5 (5 = High), to what degree are you and your students able to achieve excellence with this experience in its current form?	With which of your 5-year goals does this experience in its current form align? (i.e., M1, P2)	Write here whether you believe it is in the best interest of your students to keep, revise, or eliminate (toss) this particular activity/process.

without sufficient resources leads to decreased morale, disappointment, and lack of pride. Students know when they are doing things well and when they are not. So, if you have been doing a musical for the past 7 years, but you know that it has always been mediocre at best, you need to be honest and acknowledge this so that you can either try to make changes or plan for a new experience that might be more valuable. It is to your advantage for your students to develop tremendous pride in what they do within your program, and pride is developed when students know that they are doing something *really* well.

In the third column, you will need to write which of your goals from Table 5.2 would be furthered by that particular experience/activity/process. The purpose of this exercise is to help you think about the larger picture of what you want for your students and your program with regard to every experience that you plan. If you have done something for years (an annual holiday concert, a music theory unit) but find that it doesn't really relate to the current goals you have for your program, then you should reconsider it.

In the final column, you will need to make some decisions. In light of the stakeholder expectations you outlined in Table 5.1, the resources you currently have, and the goals that you have set for your program in Table 5.2, which of the musical experiences and processes that you list should be kept, which should be revised, and which should be "tossed"? As you consider each musical experience or process, remember that you don't have to keep doing something just because it has always been done, nor do you need to keep doing something because it is part of someone else's definition of a "successful program." Your priority is your students. What experiences will you keep from Table 5.3 because they lead to excellence, align well with your goals, and meet your students' needs and the needs of important stakeholders? Are there things you need to re-evaluate, because you do not have sufficient resources to achieve excellence? We simply cannot do everything, as Ramon reminds us:

> The hard part is balancing everything. And it's really tough, because, as a teacher, you want to do everything. I want to do everything and I can't. Even Superman can't do it all. But I think that if you set goals every year, that this year I'm going to work on such and such a thing, it will happen. Last year, my goal was to get a harp for our program, just so that would be included in our curriculum. We actually got three harps. That's been my goal, and I knew it would take me a couple years to do it. I think if we just set a pace and set goals, little by little you'll get it. Not everything can happen in your first year, but in 8 or 10 years you can be able to do it and build a program.

At the end of this process, you should have made some important decisions about your program that could lead to better learning opportunities for your students and invigoration of your program. Even if you have decided to make no changes, simply going through the process of envisioning your goals and evaluating your resources should have clarified your priorities.

Now, you can work on new ideas that you've never done before. A great place to start when imagining new ideas is your list of resources, as this can remind you of opportunities for expansion. Are there any resources that are not currently being used to their fullest? Are there new ideas that you could come up with that would better utilize the resources you currently have in place? For example, I taught in a high school where the middle school feeder system was unreliable. Aside from one consistent middle school, I never knew exactly who I would have in my band/orchestra each fall because our district had an open-enrollment option, and my students came from various middle schools from all over the district. Recruiting for my program was therefore difficult, and I worried about my student numbers declining. However, many non-band/orchestra students in the high school thought that my marching band was really great—it was a visible and popular group at the school. So, to utilize that resource, I recruited many of those students to begin an instrument in ninth, tenth, or eleventh grade in a beginning instrumental music class. Through this beginning class, many terrific high school students learned to play an instrument in one year (and to do it rather well!), and I could then involve them the next year in not only the marching band but also the concert band, jazz band, and orchestra, which provided built-in recruiting for my program. Again, it's important not to get stuck on what we don't have in terms of resources (lack of consistent middle school feeder programs and opportunities for recruitment) but to build on what we do have (excited, motivated high school students who just never had th opportunity to pick up an instrument) and come up with ideas that will help us achieve our goals (a high school beginning instrumental class).

There are many other ways that you might utilize existing resources to develop new experiences for your students. For instance, Martha decided to offer band, choir, and a new rock ensemble at her school in addition to traditional general music offerings because her students were motivated to learn an instrument and play popular music. Ramon developed a mariachi program to utilize the tremendous resource of cultural richness that his students held. We need to think outside the box rather than trying to fit into a mold of what we think traditionally denotes "success" within our programs. If developing a series of community "pop" concerts at the local park works for your students and aligns with the resources available to you, then do it. If a collaborative musical with the fifth grade teachers works, do it as well. Do what works best for *your* students, *your* program, and *your* community.

If you have other ideas for which you don't currently have sufficient resources, you can now strategically work to identify what you will need to be successful at these new activities. Document what you need (use the tables to help you!) and approach your stakeholders to outline your needs. Sometimes, they will help you find the necessary resources, and other times, you will need work to secure these resources yourself (see the next chapter for ideas from the teaching panel). Either way, it is easier to secure necessary resources when you have done a systematic examination of your program and have already thoughtfully considered how to better utilize existing resources.

Finally, I have a suggestion for adding energy, excitement, and richness to your newly revitalized curriculum. The final step that you can take is to "dream big" with regard to one exciting new experience that you can implement in the next year or two. I call this your "Dream Idea." For now, forget about the resources you currently have available. If there was one exciting, imaginative thing you could do with your students to energize and revitalize your program in the next year or two, what would it be? Would you take a big trip to perform someplace your students have never been? Would you purchase a class set of ukuleles and start a ukulele ensemble? Would you start an after-school multicultural ensemble, where students play and sing the music of various cultures? Would you purchase a set of tablets and develop a unit on composing music for video games? Would you bring in two wonderful clinicians every year to lead a weekend retreat with your students? Would you attend a professional development workshop on West African drumming and purchase instruments so that you could develop a drumming program with your students?

There are so many exciting things that you could do with your program, but to make this achievable, manageable, and realistic, start with just one big dream idea. Once you have an idea, try to list all of the new resources you would need to achieve that one goal. Try to get your principal or administrator excited about this one dream idea. Once you have their support (for this one idea!), talk with parents and community members and ask them to help you find the needed resources to make this a reality. If you can focus on one exciting new idea to start, gather appropriate resources and put it into place, it can get your students and community excited about what you are doing. Their excitement can create momentum and enthusiasm about your music program, which will later allow you to implement more new ideas down the line. Often, it is just that one first project that gets the ball rolling. What will you dream up? What can you and your students do?

In summary, at the end of this process, you should be able to answer the following questions:

1. What aspects of your current program would you like to keep, because they are working well?
2. What aspects of your current program would you like to "revise" because they have potential to work well but need new resources or a better design?
3. What aspects of your current program should be discontinued because they do not lead to a culture of excellence nor align with available resources?
4. What new ideas would you like to implement that will align well with existing resources or for which you could seek additional resources?
5. What is one innovative, creative "Dream Idea" that you can imagine for your students that you can work to develop in the next two years, for which you will seek new resources?

If you can answer these questions, you are well on your way to contextualizing your urban music program to better meet the needs of your students and community. You can type the answers to these questions in proposal format and give them to your administrator in order to begin a dialogue about how you would like to strengthen the learning experiences of your students, or use this process informally to inform your own goals. In the end, the goal of this process is to develop learning experiences that lead to musical and personal student success and promote a structure to support student excellence. Martha reminds us that our job is to "set it up so that your students are successful at each tiny step of the way." To get there, the final piece of the puzzle is figuring out how to motivate our students to achieve success with the goals and activities that we have planned.

MOTIVATING OUR STUDENTS TO ACHIEVE

Suppose we have designed terrific, innovative, and impactful musical experiences for our students and have secured the needed resources to help them achieve their goals, but are still having trouble getting them invested in or excited about the music program. We may have a problem with motivation. Motivation is an important concept for every urban music teacher to consider because it is the "energy" that we need to drive and promote a culture of excellence within our program. Of course, motivation is relevant to all music teachers, not just those who teach in an urban setting. However, as issues of motivation frequently intersect with issues of cultural conflict, as described in earlier chapters, it may be an issue of particular interest to urban music educators. When students feel respected and valued within the classroom, they often demonstrate a higher level of motivation within our schools. However, when students and teachers experience cultural conflicts (for example, confusion about unstated behavioral "rules" of the classroom), motivation problems often emerge. Milner states the following:

> Cultural conflicts sometimes result in a resistant, oppositional, or confrontational environment in which educators are fighting to control students and to exert their power, and students do not want to feel controlled. Students can similarly work to be heard and to have some power in the classroom. Consequently, educators and students can work against each other, which can leave students feeling that their preferences are insignificant, disrespected, irrelevant, or subordinate to educators and to classroom/school life. As a result, students may refuse to engage in the classroom culture or refuse to learn. (Milner, 2010, p. 24)

These types of cultural conflicts must be recognized and addressed before students will begin to find increased motivation within our classes.

How do we motivate our students to achieve their potential within our program and in other areas? People who have studied motivation for years state that there is no such thing as a non-motivated student, but there are plenty of students who are not motivated to work hard or do well in what *we* deem important: school, music class, band, orchestra, choir, or other areas. Often, the choices that students make, the effort that they devote, and the persistence that they show within our classrooms can be explained by motivation.[1] One of the problems that all music teachers face in getting our

---

1. I am grateful to James Austin, professor of music at the University of Colorado, for inspiring many of the topics in this section with his February 2013 lecture entitled "Into the Black Hole: Exploring Motivation Constructs and Implications for Music Learning."

students motivated to work hard, to practice, and to become better musicians is the common misconception that music is a talent, or inborn capability, that is given to some who are then naturally able to be musical. The problem with this perspective on musical ability is that it greatly diminishes the role that hard work and diligent practice play in the development of any musician's abilities and skills. We need to educate our parents and our students to the malleable nature of musical ability and stress the role that hard work plays in becoming a good musician. We can do this in many ways, such as by bringing in local musicians who discuss the journey that they took to become a musician or by holding workshops on how to practice.

Research demonstrates that students begin to develop beliefs at an early age (as early as first grade!) about whether they are good at math, or music, or any other specific subject (Marsh, 1984). These beliefs about their abilities often form before students have had any chance to develop their skills, and they can be quite powerful. Students' self-concept about how good they are as musicians will greatly affect how motivated they are to study the subject in our classrooms. If students come into our music classroom believing that they are not musicians, or that they are just "not good" at music, they will obviously have little motivation to work hard in our classes. In fact, some students who hold a negative self-concept as musicians or who fear failure will employ a skill called "self-handicapping" (Feick & Rhodewalt, 1997; Kolditz & Arkin, 1982): they will purposefully choose tasks that are too easy or hard, withhold effort, deflect responsibility, discontinue participation, and debase the subject or activity. For students who are exhibiting these types of behaviors in our music classrooms, we need to focus on the development of their skills, giving them extra instruction, perhaps, in a low-risk atmosphere (i.e., after-school lessons, group rather than individual improvisation sessions) and helping them to establish a set of progressive goals (i.e., gradually increasing a metronome marking week by week or playing the simple outline of a bass line on an Orff instrument on the path to gradually adding other notes) that will get them to see that success is indeed possible.

Motivation is also enhanced when students gain confidence in what they are doing. As teachers, we often try to encourage and motivate our students by providing them with positive affirmations (Great work on that countermelody, tenors! What an elegant ending to your composition, Lucy!). Such affirmations can contribute to a positive classroom culture, which is very important. However, such affirmations can also be perceived as hollow if they are not accompanied by genuine success built on a history of challenge and risk. So how do we as teachers try to motivate our students in ways that will matter? According to music education researcher Jim Austin (2013), we need to do the following:

- Build student self-concept upon a history of genuine and meaningful accomplishments (bedrock, not quicksand);
- Teach toward and recognize diverse forms of musicianship (music ability is multifaceted); and
- Provide students with honest and balanced feedback (praise the act, not the child, identify strengths as well as areas needing improvement, and provide strategies for how to improve).

Although a student's beliefs about how successful he or she is with music (or any other subject) plays a role in how motivated he or she may be to study it, there is another important issue at play, and that is how much the student perceives that subject as being interesting, or how much he or she values that subject within the greater scheme of life (Eccles et al., 1983). The great news is that we teach a subject matter that is almost universally motivating to kids—music! Listen to your students in the hallways or just before they come in your classroom door: many of them can be heard talking about music that they listen to, or they can be heard humming or singing certain songs that appeal to them. See them after school, and almost every child will spend some part of the day listening to music. Just because a student doesn't appear to be motivated to study the kind of music that we deem important in the exact manner that we deem appropriate does not mean that the particular student isn't interested in or motivated by music. It could mean that we have to find ways as teachers to discover what kinds of music and musical activities *are* motivating to that child, and build from there.

When we find that our students are lacking in individual interest in doing well in our music classes or in being a part of our performance ensembles, research tells us that we need to work on developing "situational interest" (Chen, Darst, & Pangrazi, 2001) by introducing novelty, vividness, relevance, intensity, or choice; expanding students' palette of experiences; and helping them and ourselves to move outside of our comfort zone. This is why the planning that we did previously in this chapter is so important—remember your "Dream Idea"? Something imaginative and creative that you hoped to begin at your school in the next two years? Such an educationally appropriate, well-designed, innovative, and interesting activity/course/unit/ensemble/assignment can help students find situational interest in your program, leading them to increased motivation (see sidebar, Motivating Your Students to Be Their Best).

SIDEBAR: MOTIVATING OUR STUDENTS TO BE THEIR BEST

HOW DO YOU MOTIVATE YOUR STUDENTS TO ACHIEVE SUCCESS WITHIN YOUR MUSIC PROGRAM?

Ramon

Well, we perform a lot. We are a performance group, and I think that, just like a test or an assessment, it's important to have those goals of performance. So, in my beginner class, every six weeks we have a performance, even if it's just for a senior center, even if it's at the mall, it doesn't matter. Another thing that we do a lot is we have performance tests where I put all the names in a hat and every Friday we pick a name out and we go, okay, we're going to test everyone on measures 1 through 12. If a student doesn't play it correctly, he or she gets to do it over again the next day and the next day until its's correct. So I think by just having a friendly competition and making the students know that they're not going to be laughed at if they make a mistake and that everyone is on an equal playing field, it makes the classroom environment so much better.

Martha

Because I taught a lot of students and was a traveling teacher, my whole thing was that I needed to know student names. That was the most important thing. If I wanted a kid to do something, "Hey, you" was not going to cut it. So they made a name tag that they set up on their desk every day when I would come in. As soon as I would come in to the classroom, I would play a piece of music. That immediately set the tone to let them know that it's music class now. Then I got cardstock, and we'd fold it in half. We handed out the cards, and then I used those cards as a motivating factor: I gave stickers and stamps on the back of them to students when they would participate. I had an envelope of cards for each class. The students really seemed to enjoy that and it kept them motivated during music class.

Deanna

Performance is always a big motivator for many of my students. A big part of the year for the performing groups is festival, because there's a focus on that within the district. When I started, I was really kind of anti-festival, but I found a way to make that work and be a real motivator too. Going to state festival and being successful is a big, big deal to a middle school kid. For our more advanced students, we also do Solo and Ensemble festival, which is a big motivator. Also, live performance is a way to motivate, so we go to the Sphinx competition and they see a 13-year-old who looks like them on stage playing the Mozart violin concerto. Just to be exposed to that is so important, and I see that practicing really picks up at those times.

Eric

One of the things I did with my students that was really critical was to take them to see other successful choirs. I took them to see these incredible high school ensembles because they don't know what they're capable of if they've never seen it. Once they saw that, I said, this could be you. The only difference is not that they are a selective enrollment school or have other resources. No. The only difference is that they have the opportunity to do this work and they worked their tails off. Beyond that, I don't feel like I do very much to motivate them at all. I feel like they're motivated themselves. I think what I've done is to give them as much of a voice as possible in the program. I tell them routinely that this is not my choir—this is your choir. We have many, many, many opportunities for student leadership, and they take on those responsibilities and those organizational tasks. They take care of the recruiting and they take care of teaching many of our younger, more inexperienced students and our beginners. It's a very student-centered program. I think that when you give students the opportunity to develop something of their own, and take a really meaningful role in creating those goals and figuring out how to reach those goals, instead of just spoon-feeding them everything, they respond.

Victoria

I found that the best way to motivate students was to perform. Why would anybody practice if he had no reason to practice? If you only did two performances a year, the students would only practice when it was time for performance. I learned as I went along that we had to do more things. So I went to the nursing home next door and we started doing extra performances. The trips are also awesome to motivate the children because it's not just about going on the trips. It's what it takes to get there—it's setting a goal and learning what it takes to achieve it. When we were fundraising for our trip to London, I had a saying for the students: "What you believe, you can achieve." We raised $315,000 to go to London. It's about teaching children. I use a lot of poems to motivate and teach them. I also use music that is inspirational, either something that's on the radio or older things like "The Greatest Love of All," "Hero," or "Look within Yourself." Our children need that.

However, although novel, exciting, and interesting activities will initially draw students to our programs, in the long run, children will stay in our classes because they value what they do musically, find it interesting, and discover that it relates to what they see as being important to their lives. In the end, we need to ask ourselves—are we providing highly engaging opportunities for students to have profound experiences with music? Or are we using constantly using repetition in an attempt to quickly foster "higher, faster, and louder" musical achievement?

Finally, it is important that we carefully examine the level of challenge that students find within our program and classes. Csikszentmihalyi (1990) found that motivation is enhanced when there is a match between skill and challenge. According to his theories, when we offer too high a level of challenge or risk (i.e., by programming music that is too difficult for our students to eventually perform with success, or asking students to sing individually in front of one another without sufficient preparation), students become anxious, and their level of motivation to work at the task decreases. When we offer a level of challenge too low (by having students improvise only with a blues scale for too long, or perform the same music year after year at the end-of-year assembly), students become bored, and their motivation drops yet again. So it is important for us to consider the level of challenge that our students perceive within our classes.

To determine this, we can give students simple surveys asking questions such as "How challenged do you feel in this class?" or "Is the music we play or sing too easy, or too hard, overall?" It may be that different students in our classes are having different experiences: some advanced students may be feeling bored while others who are lagging behind may be feeling more anxious. Sometimes, we won't know who is feeling what until we ask. Once we identify them, we can create more opportunities for challenge to our advanced students (asking them to peer teach, offering extra credit for alternative assignments, allowing them to prepare solos or small ensembles to play between large ensemble performances at a concert, arranging alternative advanced parts for the pieces that we are already playing, etc.) and provide more developmentally appropriate experiences for our struggling students (i.e., simplifying difficult rhythms, pairing students with a more advanced partner, finding simple folk songs that students can sing or play with success). Eventually, we can hope to provide an optimal level of challenge that leads our students to increased levels of motivation.

Motivation matters when it comes to learning. If we are dealing with a lack of student investment in our program, are experiencing declining enrollment rates, or believe that our students lack enthusiasm for our subject matter, we need to look more closely at how we can increase motivation. There seems to be a sort of momentum that starts when we get even a few previously unmotivated or disconnected students to find interest in our program and subject—those students can begin to influence others, who influence still others, until we have a critical mass of students with whom we can truly start to revitalize and reinvigorate our program. In doing so, we can hope to improve the learning experiences of all of our students.

As music teachers and administrators of our music programs, we are responsible for designing a curriculum that fosters our students' learning through profound musical experiences. In order to contextualize our program to meet the specific needs and strengths of our students, we need to spend some time reflecting on and re-evaluating the experiences and processes that we provide. With the primary goal of improving student learning always in mind, we need to consider the expectations of important stakeholders, take inventory of current resources, establish revised goals, and consider ways to motivate our students to achieve their best.

CHAPTER 6
Common Issues of Interest for Urban Music Teachers

As urban music teachers, we encounter many of the same pedagogical, curricular, and administrative issues that our suburban and rural colleagues do. However, the ways that these issues are manifested within a particular school may depend a great deal on the socioeconomic status of the students' families, the level of bureaucracy within that school or district, the demographic makeup of the student body, and the level of resources provided to the school and the music program. In light of these issues, the strategies that urban music teachers might employ to better the learning experiences of their students may differ from those that may be successful in other settings. In this chapter, I outline several issues that urban music educators might find important: financial and material resources, administrative support, scheduling of music classes, and the implementation of various educational reforms. I also include a list of resources on a number of other topics in which you might be interested. For each of the main issues that I highlight in this section, I have asked the panel of urban music teachers to provide practical insights or strategies that they think will be helpful. I hope that reading these teachers' own experiences with and advice on these issues is helpful to you as you assess your own music program.

In discussing these issues and providing tips and ideas on how to address them, I do not mean to imply that music teachers alone are responsible for resolving them. Indeed, urban music teachers are usually incredibly busy with curricular and pedagogical activities, and it is rather appalling, for example, that most urban music teachers are forced to find ways to fundraise just to afford basic curricular materials to support their students' learning. It is also problematic that many urban music teachers are constantly having to convince administrators and other important stakeholders of the educational importance of music classes. That being said, however, the reality is that many of us have to deal with these issues; therefore, we should be prepared to do so effectively.

FINANCIAL AND MATERIAL RESOURCES

Differences in school funding structures have often led to the under-resourcing of urban districts and programs. Such financial inequalities have seriously impacted the educational opportunities for urban students, not only in music education programs but across all disciplines. Stories of poorly equipped classrooms and teachers with few resources for purchasing even basic supplies abound in urban schools. In my 2008 study of instrumental music teachers in Chicago (Fitzpatrick, 2008), I found that these teachers most commonly mentioned financial support and increased funding as the top need for their music programs.

This resonates very clearly with me. I remember asking about my budget when I first took the job in Columbus and being told that there wasn't any funding at all provided by the school. If we needed anything, we were to raise the money ourselves. I was in disbelief, wondering how I could possibly manage not only to teach my students but also to lead fundraising on a massive scale so we could function at a basic level as a program. It was a shock, to say the least, but I was young and inexperienced and accepted this as just another reality of music teaching. Through the years, we raised a lot of money, enough to fund the program and even take our performance groups on large trips every two years. However, the reality of our financial needs forced us to hold fundraisers constantly, which was tiring and challenging for me, my hard-working students, and my supportive booster group. When schools do not give music programs even basic educational materials such as sheet music (while providing textbooks and materials for all other classes), students are the ones who lose out.

For urban music programs to succeed, they need sufficient financial support and adequate resources. However, to assume that "throwing money at the situation" is a quick fix for improving the educational quality of our urban programs is unrealistic and greatly underestimates the complexity of the urban context. A successful music program has many components. Financial support is a necessary, but not sufficient, condition for developing a thriving urban music program:

> Ideally, we would like all teachers to have the best available resources and all students access to exemplary music programs regardless of the schools they attend. But it is clear that the former does not necessarily result in the latter. Adequate facilities and good instruments, for example, are not sufficient to make an ensemble sound good. They do, however, help, and so we should strive to ensure that all students in all schools have the same opportunity to access them. (Costa-Giomi, 2007, p. 57)

Next, our urban music teachers discuss the challenge of dwindling financial or monetary resources and offer advice for music teachers who may be confronting this issue.

Ramon

A lot of the families in my school are at the poverty level, and for them to rent an instrument is generally impossible. It can cost $30 to $40, so forget about it. But you can use the resources that you have. My Latino parents, they love to cook. You might say, okay, our parents could make tamales or enchiladas and have a Mexican food night. We also need to connect with the community and our partners and get them involved. Find the funding out there. Hit every Rotary club and every service club out there and say, we're starting this program for kids that are in need, kids that are not usually attracted to the mainstream music program. Sometimes, in the mainstream music program, it's just the more affluent kids that get to participate in music, and that's not what public school is all about. It should be an equal playing field. Shake the tree. Let them know. Beat the drum and tell them how great this program is for kids.

Martha

What was successful for me was to go out and find my own money and not sit there and expect them to hand me a budget and say, here's $10,000 to go spend on whatever you want to spend it on. It's not going to happen. I've become a pretty good grant writer. I've received a lot of money through "Donors Choose." I've written grants to bring things into the school. I estimate that I've had about a quarter of a million dollars' worth of donor funding in the 10 years that I've been here. That helps you to get a lot of job security because administrators know you're not coming in just to ask them to do more work. If you come in and tell them, oh, look. I've got a donation for you, administrators respond to that. I think another thing is not to expect a blank check. Don't say, do I have a budget? Instead, go in and say, you know what, here's what I'd like to do. I have this specific goal in mind, and if I had these resources to get us these instruments or whatever the project is, then here's how I think it would help the school.

Deanna

I think it's important right when you get to the job to find out in a friendly way from your administrator whether there is any sort of money for a budget, and have a budget already prepared. Ask other colleagues what they've spent and say, these are the things that I will need to run my program. Try to get some funding from the start. Maybe the response will be that we don't have a budget, and then you can take it from there. But I think that it's really important to let an administrator know that these are things that are required for the program to succeed and get running. And then it's helpful to do something like an annual big fundraiser. For example, we have our annual dance, which is a huge fundraiser and it's almost like a business within itself. So the students are being really entrepreneurial about raising money. It's its own little culture. All of that has to be approved, of course, through administration.

Eric

Number one, you don't need money to teach choir. You can do your own choral arrangements. You can go to various choral wiki sites and get free music. So it's not essential. It sure is helpful. There are opportunities to build your program without money. But when you need money, fundraising is huge. It can be a real challenge in poor communities because you're just not going to sell a $35 coupon book—that cash isn't lying around with these families. So, what works better for us is small-scale fundraising, like selling 50 cent bags of chips, and that sort of thing. I also think it's important to push for funding from your administration. They fund science, they fund math, history classes, textbooks for all these other classes. They get textbook money, and my choir got nothing at all. So it's important to just draw comparisons to what all these other programs receive and make sure the administration knows that a choir course is relatively cheap by comparison. And again, involving students in that advocacy is important.

Victoria

I've taught in programs where they didn't give me any money. Nothing. They call me the fundraising queen because I always have ideas. I've done some of everything that's legal to raise money! We sell M&M's and water outside, and those are the best ones. It works great, if the administration will allow you to do it. I've also been allowed to have a store in my school and sell snacks and things before and after school, and sometimes during the day. We also made up a cookbook, a band cookbook, where everybody has a recipe. It cost $1 to get your recipe in the book, and the book costs $10 to buy. The graphic arts students in the vocational program produced the book—they even won an award for it. I just do some of everything. We also get a lot of donations. One time the local news came out because I was trying to raise money for uniforms for my high school, and the reporter saw my instruments and said, "Oh, my God. She's got these dilapidated instruments." And this reporter said, I want to help you get instruments. So he did. He went on the news, and Conn gave me three new tubas and sousaphones, and people from all over brought me instruments for my program. I'll also go to the pawn shop and cry and tell them I only have $100 or $150 and I need three instruments, and I'll get them. I do what I have to do. One of my students was on his way to college and he didn't have a clarinet, so I went to the pawn shop. My student teacher and I tried out seven different instruments and found one that worked, and I got him a decent clarinet for $50. So that's what I do. If I have a student, I'm going to make sure they have an instrument, whatever I have to do. I'm going to make it work.

ADMINISTRATIVE SUPPORT

Some of us have been fortunate to have administrators who understand what we do and offer support for all aspects of our music program. Others haven't been so lucky. In either case, building a positive relationship with administrators should be high on the priority list of most music teachers. Because of the tremendous pressure resulting from policy mandates and school reform laws, our principals and other administrators are increasingly having to manage complex school structures in a high-stakes atmosphere. Unfortunately, music and the other arts often get lost in this administrative shuffle. As music is rarely a tested subject, and music and the arts are rarely tied to school-wide assessments, many administrators who do not understand or have never themselves experienced the important role of the arts in a well-rounded education may offer less support to our programs than we need to be successful.

This is not to blame administrators—indeed, they can be wonderful partners in a great music program. However, the relationship with administrators needs to be fostered like any other relationship. Having a terrific level of support from your administration is vital to the success of your music program. Often, most of the school-provided funding for music programs comes from an administrator's discretionary funds, and administrators can play a large role in other important issues, such as developing a supportive culture for the arts, providing priority consideration for scheduling, and fostering the support of colleagues and parents. Administrators that do this well are to be treasured, as they do our students a great service. They also do us a service as teachers, as our job satisfaction has been found to correlate with the level of administrative support we perceive for our music program (Fitzpatrick, 2008). To ensure this support, music teachers must become their own advocates and take on the challenge of "educating their administrators about what a balanced, sequential program of music instruction entails" (Smith, 2006, p. 64). Teachers who feel that their administration is not providing the necessary support for developing an excellent music program need to find ways to make connections, foster relationships, and educate administrators about the importance of what we do.

I was fortunate at Northland to have had two principals who were exceptionally supportive of my program. Both recognized the instrumental music program as one of the most successful classes/organizations in the school. We received positive press, we performed throughout the community, and we garnered a great deal of positive attention, which was especially important in a school that often received only the opposite. Both of my principals even gave up several of their school breaks to go on major trips with me and my program, just to support us—I was incredibly lucky! But I also worked hard to foster that relationship, stopping in to chat with them often, publicly thanking my administrators at concerts and events, and inviting them to visit my rehearsals and classes. I remember one of my principals frequently coming into my band room first thing in the morning just to sit, watch my rehearsal, and listen to my group play. He said that it was the best part of his day. I cannot stress how much this meant to my students—how proud they felt! I also felt that just by sitting in my rehearsal, he learned a great deal about what I was teaching and what my students learned every day. I am positive that this helped him to better appreciate the importance of our subject.

For those who do not have such support, or for those looking to build an even better relationship with their administrators, our teachers have a few words of advice.

Ramon

I'm a big champion of my program. My students are always in the newsletter, on television, on the radio because I think as teachers we don't brag enough about our programs or our kids. You're not bragging about yourself as a teacher, you're bragging about the kids! So if you take your program and champion it to the community, your administration can't touch you. You have to make your program untouchable and say, look, our program's here, we've got 100 kids—it's all about the numbers, of course—I have 100 kids, and they all want to be part of this program, but I have kids without instruments, and I need your help.

Martha

Nine times out of ten, you are the music expert, so you have to educate everybody in the building as to what we do, and that includes your principal. Administrators may not understand the work that goes into putting on a show or the academic value of what goes into what we do, and they have to be educated. It takes a long time and it's a very slow process sometimes, but you have to very kindly educate the people that you work for so that they'll support you. If they weren't successful in music class, then they're not going to believe in it. So you have to show them. Too many teachers have this adversarial position against the administration, and half the time the administration is just as frustrated as we are—they're not the enemy.

Deanna

Do a special invite to a special class that you're having, and honor them in some way, like composing a special song for them in their honor. I mean, flattery is always a really good way to win people over, right?

Eric

I think the most important thing to do is to advocate for what the students need and deserve. Nothing in my program would happen without the support of my administration and my colleagues, but it took years to get them on our side. Finding a way to advocate for your needs and to demonstrate why their support is so important before such a program even exists is a big challenge. With my administration, I said, look, we can be ambassadors for our school. In urban education these days, the principals are having to deal with a lot of competition—competition with charter schools and privatization and all of that. So I sold it as a way for our school to reach out to the community—I said, you can do that with the choir, and it's cheap, and inexpensive, and it builds a sense of community. Administrators don't necessarily think of that. But our students did most of the advocating, not me. Always, always, always frame the need for a program and the need for the support to build a program in terms of what the students need. It's not about what I need. It's not about what anybody else in the school wants. It's about the kids. The best way to get them on your side is to advocate for your students.

Victoria

Sometimes administrators just don't understand what we deal with, so we have to educate them. Before the principal that I have now went to London with us, she thought that I had all the smart kids in the band and that all my kids in the band were well-off. She didn't know that I have poor children. She didn't know that I had children who were hurting—children who would act out and strike out at the people they love. She didn't realize this. She thought everything was just fine down there. She didn't know the things I had to go through. So taking her with us on that trip gave her quite an education, and when we came back, she supported us more.

SCHEDULING

To be successful, music programs need to be given consideration within a school's system of scheduling. Most music programs encompass multiple classes, whether they are general music classes or performance ensembles. At the elementary level, a music teacher will often work with every student in the school, and so scheduling adequate time for music classes can be challenging. Similarly, many performance classes that begin in the elementary or middle schools are "pull-out" classes that are scheduled during other classes. Research has shown that pulling students out of other classes for music is not detrimental to their success in those classes (Wallick, 1998), but arranging these schedules can be complicated.

At the secondary level, the typical American middle or high school usually offers many different ways to be involved in music. For example, my instrumental music program offered marching band, two levels of concert band, string and full orchestra, jazz band, AP music theory, and two classes of beginning instrumental music instruction. I wanted interested students to take the classes most relevant not only to their interests but also to their skill level and instrumentation, and developing a schedule for this was complex. The situation can become especially complicated with regard to the student schedules of both low- and high-achieving students, who are often required to take either remedial or advanced coursework that may be scheduled at the same time as the appropriate music course.

For example, in my study of teachers in Chicago, I learned that some low-achieving students were being forced to schedule double periods of reading and double periods of math so that they could improve their test scores in these areas. Therefore, a student who did not perform well on standardized tests but was, perhaps, a stellar cellist would not have had room in his or her schedule for orchestra. Some students were enrolled in Advanced Placement (AP) classes, which were frequently offered only one period a day and scheduled at the same time as music classes that were also offered only one period a day, causing some advanced students to quit playing an instrument entirely. I learned that many teachers had problems with beginners (who had never played an instrument before) and advanced musicians being mistakenly scheduled into the same ensemble class by a scheduling coordinator who simply did not know better. This situation obviously led to decreased educational opportunities for all students involved.

For elementary general music teachers who feel that they may not see their students frequently enough (or who alternate with other arts or physical education teachers to "cover" the breaks of classroom teachers), remediating this situation might necessitate a broader school-level conversation with administrators and colleagues. However, even when alternative school schedules are implemented that limit instructional time or access to music classes, music teachers can ask that the schedules of music students to be worked out first, before the rest of the students' schedules are finished. Individual school counselors may be asked to provide consideration to music students by preventing other courses which are offered only one period a day (such as advanced placement, remedial, or honors courses) from being scheduled opposite music classes. Also, the person in charge of scheduling at each school must be educated to the ways that students may be ability-grouped within different classes. For all music teachers interesting in advocating better scheduling of music courses, I recommend that you familiarize yourself with the Opportunity to Learn Standards of the National Association for Music Education (NAfME) (available both at musiced.nafme.org and in print); this publication lays out the conditions for curricular/scheduling necessary for fostering student music learning across all levels. Our selected urban teachers also have some advice.

Ramon

We do recruiting in January/February. By March, I have next year's list of students ready to schedule. You go in March to the counselors and you beat them to the game. I give them my list in March and I say, please put these kids in my classes for next year. And they're like, wow, that's six months from now, but I say, I'm giving it to you now. I think we have to be overly prepared. I think the problem happens sometimes when we go in the last week of June and say, can we put these kids in the system? No—the earlier, the better. I know you're constantly recruiting, but if we don't get in to those committees and give them the list early, then they'll say it's too late. Beat them to the game. I personally meet with a secretary or counselor and I put each student in the system name by name. So, I go with the counselor on a name-by-name basis, because I want to make sure the students get in the right class. I think that a lot of us teachers depend on the counselors too much. They've got 2,000 kids to worry about. Are they going to worry about 100 kids? I doubt it. So I think we need to go and be part of the scheduling process. I know it's not exciting to be on those committees, but if we are part of the scheduling committees and the counseling committees, when they talk about moving some music class, you can be there and you can say no. We have to be part of those committees. I know that music teachers are overworked and underpaid, but they need to be part of those committees or at least get somebody in the art program on those committees so they make sure that it happens.

Deanna

Scheduling is a headache. We have nine periods at the elementary and middle school. In my two situations in the elementary school, I taught in a pull-out program, so I got to schedule all my own classes, and that is a beautiful thing. However, you're not really considered as "legit" by the other teachers if you're doing that because sometimes it feels like you're fighting them for their time. Sometimes they seem to have an attitude like, oh, you're the music teacher that gets to pull the kids that you want to see whenever you want to see them—and aren't you special? At my middle school, I've taken on some more administrative roles in the last few years. I do the school calendar, which is really helpful for booking the auditorium and things like that. I was assigned it, but it was a good gig to have because I knew what was going on in the building at all times.

Eric

Sometimes it's hard to get our classes to be scheduled as curricular during the day. You can only do so much on the students' lunch period when they all are assigned different lunch periods. I have colleagues who have built successful after-school programs and have used that success to leverage better scheduling during the school day, because the administration can then see the value of those after-school programs. That's probably the most effective way I've seen to get both administrative support and scheduling support during the school day. You can then say, hey, look at what these kids are doing on their own volunteer time; imagine what could happen if we could do this during the day!

Victoria

Well, at the middle school, I would get to know the person who was doing the scheduling. I always butter people up that are doing scheduling. I worked with the scheduling person at the middle school, and when I learned how to do the scheduling after a few years, I started doing all the scheduling for the whole school. I was doing the class lists, and then I was able to put my students in certain classes and make sure I could get them when I needed them. Now, when I got to high school, it was really difficult getting the students I needed at the same time. So that's why I would have before- and after-school rehearsals to work on performance techniques. With the counselors, I will bring them lunch every day for the first week of school. I will butter them up so that they would give me my students in the right classes. So when I go in and ask them, can you change this student around, they say, okay, Ms. Miller. Some of them felt like the children didn't need two band classes, and that definitely they didn't need three. But the jazz band, symphonic band, and marching band are three totally different things. I mean, just different. So you have to get people to realize that. Now, another music teacher that I know told me that once a year he invites the counselors to his room during jazz band, and has lunch for them. And he has the jazz band play, and talks to the counselors about each of his classes and they are different. I was going to try that this year, but I just didn't get a chance to do it.

SCHOOL REFORMS

When I began teaching and attended my first districtwide professional development program, I remember feeling a bit overwhelmed by the topic: teaching reading within every subject. How on Earth, I wondered, was I supposed to do this in my band and orchestra classes? I remember expressing my frustration to some of the experienced teachers with whom I was sitting, who only laughed. One of them said to me, "Kate, the only thing you can be sure of in this district is that there will be some sort of new initiative every few years. Right now it's reading across the curriculum, but three years ago it was something else, and two years before that something else. Everybody's got a solution, but when it doesn't immediately produce gains in standardized test scores, they're on to something new." These experienced teachers, in a district which was then deemed as "failing," had seen educational reforms come and go, from the integrative forced busing policies of the late 1970s to the charter school movement of the 1990s and 2000s. They surely saw some of these reforms as having been helpful and others as having been disruptive or even harmful. Regardless of how we feel about each individual initiative, I believe that it is safe to say that school reform initiatives are here to stay.

Some of these recent reforms tend to focus on "back-to-basics" coursework and standardized assessment, and they have had an impact on the availability of arts programs in urban schools. Many have concentrated on the use of high-stakes standardized testing to assess students, teacher merit pay tied to various student outcomes, continuation of the charter school and school choice movements, year-round schools, project-based education, and various forms of digital education. These reforms and others come packaged with different names at different times, and many others are sure to emerge. Most of these reforms have wonderful aims, including mitigating the devastating effects of poverty and leveling the playing field for all children. As teachers, we often support these types of goals but question the means in which reforms are delivered and administered. Regardless, as educators and professionals who have been entrusted with improving educational opportunities for our students, we have to implement such policies in ways that best serve our students' needs while we are also trying to protect their interests. As each individual school reform initiative is different from the one that came before, it is impossible here to provide practical strategies for making the most educational opportunity out of each. However, we expect that urban music teachers will continue in the coming years to navigate emergent issues related to major school reform initiatives, so it is important to consider how we can ensure that these initiatives meet the needs of our students. Next, the members of our urban music teaching panel discuss their own experiences with such reforms:

Ramon

Well, we are currently implementing several initiatives. They all seem to be missing the arts. If we don't change that, we're not going to have students who will be able to think for themselves, imagine, and create, like they talk about at the end of *Mr. Holland's Opus*, right? And that's the issue, so we need to be part of those administrative committees to advocate for the arts.

Martha

It's very frustrating in this testing environment and with the constant cutting of funds for the arts. It's a constant battle, and it's a hard one to fight if you have to fight it alone. So you've got to try to find allies where you can who will support the arts and music even through these reforms. Most of these things that they're teaching us, we're already doing in music classes—it's just a matter of learning how to express it in the vocabulary in terms that they are putting forth.

Deanna

Well, I think it's important to be informed about what these things are all about. But when you walk in that building, your job is to teach music in your classroom, and that's what you need to do. At times, you're going to have to take the time to explain to others that music already teaches all of these other things that they're asking us to do. Most of the time, when an administrator comes into my room and sees what I'm doing, it kind of clicks. They get that I'm teaching all of these other things and they see that every student is engaged. With the budget cuts and emergency financial managers and reforms and everything, I don't pay a whole lot of attention, because my job there is to serve these kids and not to really worry about what's happening on that end.

Victoria

I can't worry about Detroit and the problems the city is facing. I can't worry about how the Detroit Public Schools are falling apart. My job is to teach the children how to believe in themselves, how to work hard and to know that if you work hard and believe in yourself, you can accomplish anything. Through music, I can do that—I can teach them beautiful music and how to feel good when they play. I teach them that you don't have to turn to drugs—when you're upset, play your instrument—it will relax you. If you focus on what's important, and teach your children those important things, there is nothing that can stand in your way. They won't let you go. You will always have a job no matter what.

The issues that urban music educators encounter are many and multifaceted, and this chapter includes only a few strategies for addressing some of them. The figure at the end of this chapter offers recommended readings and resources that you can consult about a host of other issues that may be of importance to you as an urban music educator. There are many more issues that are currently important to each of us, and others that have yet to evolve. When you find yourself in need of practical advice or strategies to address some of the issues not covered in this chapter, it is important that you reach out to others whom you trust, including experienced music teachers in your area who deal with the same issues, helpful colleagues of other subjects, and university professors who you trust. The urban music teaching environment is extremely complex, and there are no quick answers to many of the questions that we ask. However, this should not stop us from pursuing greater understanding of the important issues that relate to our students' growth.

Teaching English-Language Learners	**Sheltered Content Instruction: Teaching English-Language Learners with Diverse Abilities (2007)** Jana Echevarria & Anne Graves Allyn and Bacon
	English Language Learners: The Essential Guide (2007) David Freeman & Yvonne Freeman Scholastic Teaching Resources
	Getting Started with English Language Learners: How Educators Can Meet the Challenge (2007) Judie Haynes ASCD
	www.colorincolorado.org Helpful website in English and Spanish for teachers and families of English language learners (ELLs). Includes a wealth of resources for teachers of all content areas including lesson plans, resources for ELLs, special learners, technology, identification, and assessment.
Teaching Students with Special Needs	**Teaching Music to Students with Special Needs: A Label-Free Approach (2011)** Alice Hammel & Ryan Hourigan Oxford University Press
	Music in Special Education, Second Edition (2010) Mary Adamek and Alice-Ann Darrow American Music Therapy Association
	Teaching Music to Students with Autism (2013) Alice M. Hammel and Ryan M. Hourigan Oxford University Press
Working with Children in Poverty	**Reaching and Teaching Students in Poverty: Strategies for Erasing the Opportunity Gap (2013)** Paul Gorski Teachers College Press
	The Art of Freedom: Teaching the Humanities to the Poor (2013) Earl Shorris W.W. Norton
	Understanding Poverty in the Classroom: Changing Perceptions for Student Success (2011) Beth Lindsay Templeton R&L Education.

Working with Immigrant and Domestic and International Migrant Populations	**Where Do I Go from Here? Meeting the Unique Educational Needs of Migrant Students (2007)** Karen Vocke Heinemann
	DreamFields: A Peek into the World of Migrant Youth (2012) Janice Blackmore CreateSpace Independent Publishing Platform
	The Inner World of the Immigrant Child (1995) Christine Igoa Routledge
	The World of Mexican Migrants: The Rock and the Hard Place (2009) Judith Adler Hellman New Press
Fostering Parental Involvement	**Organizing Your Parents for Effective Advocacy (2008)** Kenneth Elpus *Music Educators Journal, 95(2)*
	Beyond the Bake Sale: The Essential Guide to Family/School Partnerships (2007) Anne Henderson New Press
	The Essential Conversation: What Parents and Teachers Can Learn from Each Other (2004) Sara Lawrence-Lightfoot Ballantine Books
Positive Classroom Management for Diverse Populations	**Managing Diverse Classrooms: How to Build on Students' Cultural Strengths (2008)** Carrie Rothstein-Fisch and Elise Trumbull Association for Supervision and Curriculum Development
Advocating for Your Program: Confronting Program Cuts	**Music Advocacy: Moving from Survival to Vision (2010)** John Benham R&L Education
	The National Association for Music Education's Advocacy Page http://advocacy.nafme.org

CHAPTER 7

Finding Support and Inspiration

Have you ever seen the movie *Music of the Heart*? What about *Stand and Deliver*? *Lean on Me*? *Freedom Writers*? Such movies often paint a portrait of a dedicated urban teacher fighting against the odds to "rescue" his or her students from the challenges of the urban environment. In these films, urban students are frequently portrayed as being "in need of saving." The schools are dirty and decrepit, the teachers (except for the hero or heroine) just don't seem to care, and the parents are neglectful, detached, uninvolved, and often abusive. These problems seem to exist until the arrival of a "savior," a young or new teacher who is not from the city, and usually white. Magically, this one person is able to solve all of the deep-seeded, interconnected, structural inequities faced by these students—and, of course, the students and the teacher always find their happy ending.

The stereotypes of urban schools, students, parents, and teachers embedded in these movies are incredibly problematic. Just as problematic are the unrealistic expectations provided by these dramatizations. In real life, the triumphs of an urban music teacher and his or her students are more likely to be incremental than sudden, taking place behind the scenes rather than in front of the cameras, and without terrific fanfare or immediate reward. For most of us, the biggest contributions we make to a child's life may never be recognized by anyone—not even by the child . Most of us do our most important work (counseling a frustrated teenager, buying a third grader a new coat, giving free private lessons to students who cannot afford them, developing creative and interesting lessons to capture our students' imaginations, creating musical accommodations for our students with special needs) in spaces where they can't be seen. We want so badly to do good for our students, but we also experience times when we feel burnout and frustration because change is not coming fast enough, our students are not responding quickly enough, or we do not feel supported enough by those who matter to us. We need inspiration, we need encouragement, and we need understanding. This chapter is devoted to helping you find this for yourself.

ON FINDING JOB SATISFACTION

Despite the perception that urban music teachers face more difficult situations than do others, in-service teachers within urban music education settings demonstrate relatively positive attitudes toward teaching in an urban school. Ausmann (1991) conducted surveys of urban music teachers in Ohio's seven largest urban centers to identify their attitudes toward teaching music in an urban context. These teachers indicated a surprising level of satisfaction with their teaching positions, as 72% agreed or strongly agreed that they enjoyed teaching in an urban school. In my 2008 study of Chicago instrumental music teachers, I similarly found that these teachers reported relatively positive job satisfaction levels, which were actually slightly higher than the national levels reported by music teachers across other contexts. It was also interesting see that these teachers' level of job satisfaction was correlated with how successful they considered their music program to be, how much administrators and colleagues supported them, how high they reported their expectations of their students to be, and how clean, orderly, and safe they perceived their schools as being.

What I found most interesting from the results of my 2008 study was not the teachers' average job satisfaction "score"; it was the way the teachers I interviewed described "living" their job as an urban music teacher. Although they agreed that, overall, they were relatively satisfied with their jobs, it was difficult for them to reconcile the extremes of both frustration and reward they experienced daily in their career. They discussed encountering significant challenges and frustrations every single day as urban music teachers; contributing greatly to these frustrations were scheduling conflicts, lack of resources , student behavior problems, and lack of administrative support. They also reported experiencing tremendous rewards from their jobs, most of which related to seeing students achieve great things musically and personally, and also to having former students come back to tell them how much of an impact music had made on their lives. These two factors of frustration and reward, rather than "averaging out" to produce a level of daily contentment or satisfaction with urban music teaching, were constant, daily, and polarizing presences in the lives of these teachers. Whether this is unique to urban music teachers or not, I do not know (see sidebar, Why We Do What We Do).

Many of us love our career as an urban music teacher and wouldn't trade our experiences for anything. However, this does not mean that we don't experience many days where we are extremely frustrated with some (or many!) aspect(s) of urban music teaching. Yes, we reap great rewards from the work we do. And, yes, we also experience great challenges that cause us tremendous frustrations. Some days are terrific, and some days are harder than anyone might believe. Many days, we experience both frustration and reward at the same time. Sometimes it is difficult to reconcile these conflicting emotions about our chosen

SIDEBAR: WHY WE DO WHAT WE DO

WHAT IS MOST REWARDING ABOUT YOUR CAREER AS AN URBAN MUSIC TEACHER?

Ramon

Well, the thing that keeps me going is when you turn that kid around that's not doing well in school, that's one step away from joining a gang, and you give them this instrument and it saved their life, I mean, it's like a 360-degree turnaround. You see it, and there's no greater feeling than to see a kid that you changed their lives. Or, sometimes you see a twelfth grade kid playing the violin, and you remember back when they were in sixth grade and they told you they didn't know what instrument they wanted to play, and you told them, you look like a violin player. You didn't really know at the time, but now they're one of the best violinists in the state or something like that. I see it when I have those students that are sending me their diplomas or sending me their college degrees because of this program. They say, I made it. I became a leader, and now I'm doing this and this. It just keeps you going. It's just really touching and heart-warming when the students come back to you five years later and give you a card that says, you were right.

Martha

The best thing about teaching music is the joy on any kid's face when they discover something and you help them discover it. I'm thinking in particular of my first graders who learn to play the keyboard. When they get up and they learn to put their fingers in the right place and play a song for the first time, there's just, there's nothing better, because that's something that just potentially changed their trajectory, just the ability to do that.

Deanna

Yeah, it's incredibly rewarding to have the opportunity to expose so many kids to this whole new world. I mean, it's just those moments of hearing my students play or seeing them now as college students. And then the first time the kids open up a case and go, oh, it's beautiful, I hope this is mine to play—that's also very rewarding. There's so much I can share with them, and for others to be inspired by music and love it too is great, even if they don't continue playing their instruments their whole lives.

Eric

What keeps me coming back is the impact that what I do has on students. We focus a lot on beauty and love in my choirs. We focus on how to bring those things into our lives, and to give those things to each other and to ourselves. And of course, I want my students to read music and be able to analyze music and play a little keyboard, and listen critically and reflect on their musical abilities, but most important, I want them to reflect on who they are as human beings and what value they bring to this world and a huge part of the value that they bring is beauty and love. And singing and choral music is a wonderful way for them to experience that beauty and love within themselves and to share it with other people. Every teacher has this experience, when you have those students who you've worked with for four years, and you're a bawling, sobbing, weeping mess when they graduate and they go on. And they send you a little note two or three year, or eight years later. And you just get teary eyed. And those experiences are invaluable for me, and I think for the students as well.

Victoria

I truly enjoy it. It's not a job. It's not. It's not like working. When you enjoy what you do, it's not a job. You're going to get challenges all your life. So I look back, and I can smile, and I can remember all the people who I saved and helped. I've created great students.

This year, we were at state festival, and we got a one and two twos, and the kids were a little disappointed. But one of my students was saying, I don't feel bad, he said, because I was created. He said, Mrs. Miller creates good musicians. We don't come to high school already knowing how to play. And I just said, wow. That is great to know how they feel about what I do. So I truly enjoy what I do, and I don't regret one minute of it.

careers. For example, Eric talked about the conflicting thoughts he has about his job:

> I can't think of a better career or job for me. On the other hand, I consider leaving the profession pretty much on an annual basis. Those two things might seem like they're in conflict, but for me they are not. I couldn't be happier, but I've also never been more exhausted in my life.

Part of the reason why we have such conflicting feelings about our careers is that teaching is an often all-encompassing profession:

> People snarkily mention how easy it is to be a teacher, with our many breaks and summers off. Anyone who teaches knows that this is a lie because teaching has no end. No. End. This is both a curse and a blessing. It is a curse because my mind is always in teacher mode. When I read a book, I think of how I might teach it. When I see an article in the newspaper, I assess its reading level for my students.

I lesson plan in the shower. But on the flip side is a blessing. Once you are a student's teacher, you are his or her teacher forever. (Ungemah, 2014, p. 99)

If you are a beginning urban music teacher, or are considering becoming an urban music teacher sometime in the near future, it is important to note that this struggle may be more difficult for you to reconcile than for an experienced teacher. Research shows us that at one point, approximately half of all new teachers in urban schools left within the first five years of teaching (Haycock, 1998). How do we explain this? A researcher named Jean Clandinin studies the knowledge that teachers develop through teaching and has suggested that experienced teachers may have an easier time dealing with the daily ups and downs of teaching because they have a better knowledge of the typical, almost rhythmic patterns of school life:

> In the narrative of experienced teachers, there is an annual reconstruction of experience, and it is through this cyclic repetition of school life that teachers come to "know" their classrooms rhythmically. This knowledge, recollected as they teach, allows them to cope with variations as they reconstruct a story already lived out that is appropriate to the situations they confront. This living out of the narrative is modulated rhythmically. They know the down times will be followed by up times; they know that cyclic disruptions are temporary. (1989, p. 123)

This type of rhythmic "sense of knowing" develops throughout the first few years of a teacher's career. Less experienced teachers, therefore, may have an especially difficult time dealing with frustration. They may blame themselves for many things that are beyond their control, such as exaggerated student misbehavior before spring break, problems getting students to focus during beautiful weather, or exaggerated levels of student stress before periods of standardized testing. Experienced teachers already know that these things happen, and they plan for them. This doesn't mean that experienced teachers don't feel frustration any less than do inexperienced teachers, but it does mean that they may be better able to put the challenges that they confront into context. They also may have strategies for dealing with frustrating days, as Ramon discusses next:

> Those letters or notes that students write to me, I keep them in a pile. I do. And so when I have a bad day, I'll pull them out, and I'll read them. I'll remind myself that this is why I wanted to teach. Or I'll talk to someone, or look at something that I've done with the students and have accomplished. I'd encourage others to save all those accomplishments, because sometimes you have something with your administrator that didn't go well or something with your students

that didn't go well. On those days, if you can reflect on the good things and just try to bring the good things to your mind, you'll be all right. In our profession, we're here to change kids' lives. I think you see that, even in the smallest way, we're changing kids' lives, and we're changing the direction of their life. And the good, hardworking teacher keeps that in mind every day.

Martha also describes the extreme frustration she felt in her first year as a teacher, describing how she had to get back to basics to remember the magic of teaching children:

> When I was in that first year of teaching, I was crying almost every day because I didn't know what to do. On the worst days, I would pull out something like *Green Eggs and Ham* and read it to the kids, and I had them. Even if they couldn't speak English, they were riveted. And that was when I was like, this is what I'm supposed to be doing. This is a calling. I've done all these other things and I'm glad I did them first but this is what I'm supposed to be doing.

Interestingly, while a lot of studies have looked at the challenges urban teachers face, very little research has examined the types of rewards they perceive from teaching in the urban environment. This is perplexing to me: why are the challenges of urban teaching so often discussed, as if teaching in the urban context can only be negative? As a former urban music teacher myself, I understand very clearly the challenges that are offered by teaching in an urban school. However, I wouldn't have lasted more than a day as an urban teacher if I hadn't also felt rewarded by my experiences in some way. Teaching is hard—there is no way around it. However, as urban teachers, we persist because it is our students, in the end, who motivate us to confront the challenges that we face head on in order to do our very best every day.

TAKING CARE OF YOU

Take some time right now to evaluate the current feelings you have toward your urban music teaching career. Are you feeling energized? Burned out? If you could change jobs tomorrow to do something else, would you? How is the balance between your home life and your career? How often do you get to school early or stay late to accomplish the goals you have set as an urban music teacher? How much support do you currently have from those in your personal life (i.e., significant others, family, etc.)? How much support do you currently have from those in your professional life who

really understand what you do (i.e., other urban music teachers, mentors, colleagues)?

If you find that any of your answers to these questions concern you, this is the time to take action. Your personal well-being is incredibly important to your success as an urban music teacher. Unfortunately, due to the lack of resources that urban music teachers often experience and the multiple roles that we usually take on (counselor, curriculum developer, instrument repairperson, custodian, recording engineer, set designer, etc.), the risk of burnout for us is high. We also often experience professional isolation. Many of us work extreme hours at our schools to be able to accomplish our goals. I remember being a new teacher and staying at school until 8 PM almost every night and working most weekends just to finish writing my marching band drill (for which we couldn't afford a drill designer) and to complete administrative tasks such as bus requisitions and program design. I remember worrying about whether I would ever be able to have a family while working such long hours (an unacceptable dilemma!), but I didn't understand how to do my job any other way. If I didn't do it, no one would. Either I sacrificed my time for my students and program, or I would let my students down.

SIDEBAR: INSPIRATIONAL SUMMER READING

Jackson, R. (2009). *Never work harder than your students and other principles of great teaching.* Alexandria, VA: Association for Supervision and Curriculum Development.

Palmer, P. (1998). *The courage to teach.* San Francisco: Jossey-Bass.

Mayer, J. (2011). *As bad as they say? Three decades of teaching in the Bronx.* New York: Fordham University Press.

Draper, S. (1999). *Teaching from the heart: Reflections, encouragement, and inspiration.* Portsmouth, NH: Heinemann.

Kozol, J. (2008). *Letters to a young teacher.* New York: Three Rivers Press.

Esquith, R. (2007). *Teach like your hair's on fire: The methods and madness inside room 56.* New York: Penguin Books.

Intrator, S., & Scribner, M. (Eds.). (2003). *Teaching with fire: Poetry that sustains the courage to teach.* San Francisco: Jossey-Bass.

I didn't consider that there were other alternatives (such as delegating some of the tasks to willing parents or students), and I most definitely did not feel that I had time to spend conversing with colleagues from other schools or even—gasp!—playing my trumpet once again in some sort of ensemble once in a while. However, these things were exactly what I needed to do to be the best teacher I could be. In the following years, I learned that there is an art to working smarter, not harder. I learned that no one really seemed to notice the difference when I started working shorter hours because I began to delegate small tasks to others, but it made a huge difference in the quality of my life. Someone once told me to focus my energies primarily on those tasks that required a degree in music education to complete, because all others could usually be delegated to someone else. Even though I did not always follow that advice completely, it saved me from burnout on many occasions and helped me learn how to better value my talents and experiences.

Giving until it hurts is neither noble nor heroic—it is detrimental to us and to our ability to find balance in our lives. When we burn out, when we spend too much time working, we become bitter and we lose our enthusiasm, patience, and passion. This is not helpful for our students nor our program. If you are feeling burned out, you need to give yourself permission to let go a bit. Schedule a date with the significant other in your life.

Call or e-mail another urban music teacher and go out for coffee. Go home after school one day a week when the other teachers do. Find an ensemble to play or sing with on the weekends. Or, take some time to read some of the books listed in the sidebar on Inspirational Summer Reading. Victoria talks about how she personally finds rejuvenation after more than 40 years of teaching in the Detroit Public Schools:

> Well, you have got to come in fresh. You got to have a way to rejuvenate yourself overnight to face the children and to be able to come up with something that they didn't learn before. You've got to think outside of the box. Sometimes you might have to mentor another student teacher. I learn a lot from my student teachers—I love having student teachers. You've got to be willing to listen to other people. I have an open mind, and I'm always ready to learn. And I don't get a chance to go to as many workshops and things as I would like to go to, but when I go to things, I learn. I read some of the music magazines. I don't always have the time, but those are the things that help. You got to find ways to rejuvenate yourself. I do transcendental meditation every single morning. When I do meditation, I have more and more ideas, and I can just go, go, go, go, go. And I just need to relax sometimes because the high schoolers don't just have the energy to go, go, go like the middle school kids. So, I do it once a day. I say my prayers. I go to church on Sunday. These things help me.

For Eric, pursuing the challenge of National Board Certification was the way he sought rejuvenation:

> The National Board Certification really changed my life. You know, after three years, I was pretty burned out and I was going to quit. And I talked to a couple of colleagues who went through the national board process and they had all talked about how it sort of renewed their enthusiasm for teaching, so I figured I'm either going to quit or I'm going to try that. So I went for it, and it definitely reinvigorated my enthusiasm for teaching and was really valuable for me professionally and personally

On her path to find balance, Deanna has rediscovered the importance of taking the time to be a musician:

> Being a musician, that's something to consider too, because you go through stages of being a musician and a teacher, right? You can lose that part of yourself because you're doing all this teaching, and you never have time to do that playing. And so that's kind of coming back into my life now, and I'm rediscovering

it. I think that's something you can lose along the way, but you have to guard against that because that comes through in your teaching too.

You must take care of yourself, personally and professionally. We do not do easy work—we do important work. Investing in and taking care of yourself needs to be an important and primary part of your plan for becoming the very best urban music teacher that you can be.

FINDING INSPIRATION

What is the impact of an urban music teacher's work? What does it all mean? Why are we doing what we are doing? In the end, I believe that most of us do what we do because we believe in the power of music to be transformative in students' lives. We usually believe this because at some point, music made a difference in our own life, whether by adding beauty, providing motivation, allowing for creativity, expanding opportunities, deepening understanding, or teaching us lessons that would have been harder to learn in other ways. The power of what we do easily gets lost under stacks of purchase orders, after-school rehearsals, professional development meetings, and chaperone duties. But it is always there, and what matters most to music teachers is whether they have been able to make a difference in the lives of their students through the power of music. Because there are no quick rewards in our profession (it sometimes takes years before a student comes back to tell us how much we meant to their lives), it is easy to become disillusioned.

To combat this, I have chosen to end this book with quotes from former urban music students. I collected the following quotes from adults who once attended urban music programs of all kinds. I am sure that just about any one of these quotes could have been written by any of a multitude of urban students whose lives have been touched by the force and beauty of music in classes just like yours. All of these quotes are impressive testaments to the power of music, music teachers, and music programs in the lives of urban students.

Perhaps you have been fortunate enough to hear these same types of things from your own students, current or former, and have been revitalized and energized by what your students have had to say. I hope that you will then read these quotes with a fond familiarity, and as you read you will recall the faces of those students you have touched in your music classrooms or ensembles. Perhaps you have not yet had the opportunity to receive such feedback from your own or former students—we have all been there. For now, "borrow" these quotes as evidence that what you do will matter tremendously to many people who desperately need you to stay encouraged, stay positive, and keep working as hard as you can to provide the best possible musical experiences for them, even in the face of obstacles. Happy reading.

Being a part of an urban music education program impacted my life tremendously. As an immigrant from Vietnam, I was always the quiet girl that was too shy and too scared to do anything at school. It was hard for me to adjust to the wants and need of my culture and to assimilate to the American customs. I was struggling everyday at school and at home to make sure that I was doing everything right and being a good daughter and sister. I believe that the music program that I was in allowed me to find an outlet in my frustrating world. It was something that I could go to when I was depressed, angry, and happy. I was depressed because of my family's situation and how much we were struggling to make a living. I got angry at the fact that I was doing everything that I could as a student and daughter and it wasn't good enough for my parents. I was happy because I got to make beautiful music where it could take my mind to the most amazing places. I remember one morning going to band like any other morning. Usually I could just put all my stressors behind me when I entered the band room. I was first chair flute at the time. Earlier that morning, before I came to school, my father had yelled at me about something that I didn't do. I was an obedient child and I didn't dare to talk back. When I was playing my flute, I began to cry. I had never cried in public before. I was so frustrated and sad at the situation that I let it all out. The band stopped playing and my teacher escorted me into her band office. She was so calm and caring, asking me if I was all right. She was always there for me. I cried so hard that I was barely understandable. She held me for a long time until I was okay. She let me stay in her office as long as I wanted and told me that this was a safe place I could come anytime and talk about anything. I believe that moments like this shaped my life. It allowed me to find an outlet for my frustration and enabled me to know that everything was going to be okay. Through all the struggles in my life, I attributed my growth to that one incident that drove me to be someone better. I wanted to be a better parent, a better daughter, a better person. Music is my second family, my second lifeline and it is my second home. I couldn't have been where I am today without music. I want to thank all the people that have ever given me that gift and have been a part of my life with music. Without you all and music I don't think I would be alive today.

The thing from my urban music program that I remember most and I have always felt was an advantage I've taken with me into my adult life was my exposure to different cultures. In an inner city school, there are many cultures represented, but I feel like being in the music program pushed me to interact with people from those cultures in ways I otherwise never would have. Now, as an adult, I am comfortable dealing with people of any background in any situation, something that I do not find to be true for the people I know from more affluent communities.

I think the most important thing that I took away from my high school music experience was the memory of closeness and family. I remember being brought together when one of our classmates passed away. Something that I have kept close to my heart over the years is a memory from my senior year. I had confided in my music teacher about financial issues that my family was experiencing. My mom was a single parent of three, and we had fallen on hard times and our cabinets were empty. I was stressed out with having to help with bills and food and it was taking a toll on my school life. One Saturday morning, there was a knock on the door and someone from a local grocery store asked me if I was (name withheld). I said "yes," and with that, they brought in bags and bags of groceries, filling up our cabinets. I later learned that it was my music teacher who had arranged this. Thinking of this memory brings tears to my eyes because that meant so much to me and my family. There are no words to describe the closeness of our music program. We might have been in the public school system, but we had each other. And as we all have gone down different paths in life, we are still family. Although I may not play my instrument anymore, music is still a big part of my life . . . and always will be.

We were never given the option of worrying about what we didn't have; instead we focused on what we could do with what we did have. Seeing the importance of focusing on the positive led me to look for the positive in other aspects of my life, even when situations were extremely difficult. I learned that instead of focusing on my problems, it was more important to find a support system and make positive strides toward my goals. That positive focus gave me just enough of a push, the support and the confidence to start the personal growth that continues to this day.

Best of all, I remember that it was a place where everyone belonged and everyone mattered. We were all equal, and because of that, I felt free to be myself.

It would take writing a book of my own to describe how urban music educators have changed my life. Music has been a way for me, and countless others, to escape the stress of life since an early age. My middle school music teacher was an amazing musician and educator and friend. He taught me that music can be perfect and metered and strict, but that it can also be liberating and about improvisation and good old fashioned fun. Thankfully, that idea was reinforced at our high school. The comraderie of our musicians always seemed reliable and steadfast, regardless of where we came from or who we were. It will never cease to amaze me that, on top of all the performances, practices, and fundraising, our teachers always made the effort to be so much more than just a teacher. They, and every urban music educator I've had the privilege of knowing, realize and accept the fact that their musicians may have more personal issues than students from more affluent communities, in which fundraising or the safety of their neighborhood may not have been prohibitive of their experience. More than any single memory or musical skill they helped me learn, they taught me that the music is in us all, and that it can be an amazing way to apply yourself and feel great about who you are and what you're doing.

Without the wonderful music educators I have had the fortune to work with and the encouragement from all of them, I would never have such a passion for music like I do. I did end up playing in college for a year and was constantly asked why I wasn't a music major. I ended up becoming an urban educator myself but in the area of mathematics. It was from the motivation and inspiration of not only my math teachers, but my music teachers as well that helped me make that decision. Our music program was more than a music program, it was truly a family.

Being a part of an urban music education program had an immeasurable impact on my life. Honestly, if I can have just half the impact that my music teachers had on my life and the lives of others, I will consider my life a success. In my opinion, our particular environment was a place where dreams could easily be fostered and guided, and whether they were music related or not is irrelevant. My experiences in our music program taught me a lot about music, but more than that, it provided me with amazing friends that I still keep up with, and examples in my teachers that I still very much so look up to. To this day, the people and experiences hold a huge place in my heart.

Like many of my classmates, music has left a lasting mark on my life. I couldn't seem to get enough music in my life from an early age. The other thing I couldn't seem to get enough of was self-esteem and a supportive environment at home. This theme continued through high school. Both fortunately and unfortunately for myself and urban music educators dealing with students like myself there is no shortage of adolescents with similar issues. In our program, I found a support system of other students who either knew how I felt or were ready and willing to simply help me heal and blossom into an individual. Not only did my classmates help with this, but my instructors did as well. While this may not have much to do with music it has everything to do with a music program that provides unconditional support to its students in all academic and nonacademic areas. As I write this, tears stream down my face, because it never ceases to amaze me how kind people can be when you need it the most, and I feel that being exposed to this kindness from both peers and adults helped to sculpt me into a person that is ready to give her heart to anyone who may need it at any time. Music and the love for it and love of it has allowed me kindness and patience which have given me strength in my life, allowed me to become a compassionate educator myself, and helped me to continue to give back to my community through volunteering.

I remember when we went to state competition in those horrible outfits and were made fun of by all the suburban kids and their far superior instruments . . . and my (rented from the school) instrument literally fell apart in my hands while we were warming up! My director had to fix it just in time. We did our thing and I remember how embarrassed I was, but then they posted our scores, and nobody was making fun of us then! The other thing I wanted to say is that I think that often high school music teachers get the "glory" (if there is glory to be had) but I think that having strong teachers in elementary and middle school is just as important, if not more so. I can imagine being an urban elementary or middle school music teacher can be very discouraging in some respects. For me, on a personal level, music class in those years had the most impact though. It was a place to belong, and an equalizer.

When you think of it, your music teacher is the one that is constant through those years of so much change. They really become one of your biggest fans and most trusted adults.

When my close friend passed away, it was my music family and teachers who got me through. I am so thankful for having been a part of a great music program. It not only helped me grow as a musician, but also as a person. We truly will always be a family.

Wow, so many memories were made in those four walls and on the marching field I wouldn't even know where to start . . . not only recalling them but on how they have influenced my life then and now. The moment that stands out most to me was when our band director decided we were going to play "Suite Provincial" for the spring concert my senior year. I was playing piccolo at the time and knew I was by far not the best . . . but it started with a piccolo and oboe duet. We read through the piece and after class I told him that maybe one of the other girls should play piccolo. His reply to me was NO! You can get a tuner and practice room and YOU will play that part. I thought he was making a huge mistake but said, OK, if you think so. I did what he said and worked really hard to get the part down. The night of the concert, I played my part on the piccolo and when it was over was so proud of myself. I did it. As I went on with my life I have remembered that I may not be the best and it may not be the easiest but with a little faith I can do anything I set out to do. So as I have continued in my life I do think back to that moment often and I am so thankful for that opportunity that taught me so much more than just how to play that piece of music. I am forever thankful to all of the music teachers I have had and all the little life lessons they somehow added in without us realizing at the time!

I remember my middle school music teacher coming to talk to me when I struggled keeping up in orchestra and started not coming to class because I thought I could never get the hang of the violin. And he came to my homeroom, pulled me out into the hallway and he talked to me like a normal person, yet someone who loved and breathed music. He told me that I had a musical gift and that it shouldn't go to waste. And to keep working hard and that it will come to me naturally. He hugged me and I went every single day to orchestra from that day forward. I have so much respect for that man! I realized how much one person can really change your life. And another time, a different music teacher got involved during my eighth grade year. All of us girls were arguing and fighting and yelling and he teared up and put his baton down and went into his office. He came out and told us how much he loved us all and how much talent we have and how the things now won't matter in the future. And he was right!

We hung out in the music room because our teacher let us be ourselves and never really cared how long we stayed. We knew someone was going to be in there, so rather than sit in a study hall full of strangers, we could hang out with friends in the music room. We might not all have been friends, but we all knew we could trust one another.

I just remember how we were all family. Everyone looked out for everyone else. The bond that we created is still very much alive today. The level of musical excellence that we got before we played at festival made you want to say "Yeah, I went to an inner city school and our band is still better than yours!" Music is still a huge part of my life and my kids' lives. Band was a safe haven where we came and were never judged by what we were wearing or who our friends were. Band was about the music, doing your best and never ever giving up.

Music and all of the performing arts are a place for students to be who they are in a world that many times tries to restrain individualism. In an educational system that is trying to mold all students to be the same and fit into the same uninteresting box, music provides a place where a student can be a square peg in a round hole. Not all kids are athletes or scoring a 36 on the ACT the first time, but when they are in band or choir or orchestra or theater, they can be who they are, and they can thrive. We call it a "home away from home" because it is the one, and maybe only, place where students can truly be themselves without fear of ridicule, are free to be creative, and welcome to be around other students who are doing the same. Also, in an urban setting that too often lacks structure, discipline, and leadership, our music program provided what students needed in their lives and in their development. Teaching students about being on time, having high expectations, discipline, work ethic, etc., is something that the performing arts gives urban students that the classroom sometimes cannot.

The music room was a place where we were all free to be us. We shared a common love for music, and it was that common love of music that pulled us all together. It also fostered that home away from home because we knew we had to work as a unit. Playing music is not a solo event. Also, with the music teachers there is a different bond. There is a trust and a connection that you do know you can go to them for anything. Maybe this occurs because we do spend so much of our time with them. But regardless of why or how it happens the music room is a safe zone . . . a comfy place to be.

We had no sense of disadvantage, and we actually felt more privileged than our suburban and private school peers. No amount of money would have given us the education of community, respect, or craftsmanship that we got in our program. The music program, although a haven or second home, was a safe way for us to learn about the world around us. We helped out when our classmates were struggling with health, financial, or home issues. Music education (all the arts!!!) made us better prepared to become effective educators, artists, communicators, etc. because we were exposed to so much diversity at that age.

Those of us lucky enough to have great music teachers know the difference and impact of having teachers who truly care about their students, who have a real passion for music. The same can be said about any area of study. When a student knows they are cared about, it creates that motivation to push themselves.

Where do I begin? . . . In our music program, I not only gained incredible knowledge of music, I gained a family and amazing mentors. After multiple tragedies, we all came together, whether we were in high school, or haven't talked to each other in years. We became a family, and you cannot find that anywhere else. I have the utmost support to give to anyone looking to be or who currently is an urban music teacher.

I may not have been an amazing musician, but music gave me discipline, a love for music and a desire to learn. I am 26 years old and never thought I would play my violin after high school. But almost a decade later, I am playing musicals in a church orchestra! I love playing! I'm still no child prodigy, but I play for me and the love of music that I experienced many years ago.

I've come to realize what my urban music program meant to me. I was always notorious for not ever working to my full potential, yet somehow my music teacher managed to push me in ways I had never been pushed before. I remember practicing for the musical Cinderella. I was filling in for a lead that wasn't there and had to sing a part that was not my own. She was in the pit, conducting away, and she looked up at me with that comforting smile that she had a way of giving without even knowing it and calmed me down. From that rehearsal on, she was my focal point, and I knew that she would be there, a sort of beacon in the storm, to keep me on track and in place.

I was awkward and insecure in high school, and had a lot of issues going on in my family. My father was an alcoholic and I was just realizing it as I was entering high school. He was never physically abusive but he was extremely verbal the more he drank. I was also battling an eating disorder, I hated myself. Music was the only thing I had a talent for. I wasn't into sports, my grades were good but not the best, and I was well liked in school but didn't fit into any of the groups. Music was my only outlet for pain, fear, anxiety, anger, and happiness. I could play for hours, and it was the only way I could express myself. Our program itself was also one big family. My music teacher helped me more than she will ever know. She was the only person I could talk to about everything in my life. She was a mentor, and showed me how to be confident and believe in myself. She gave every student an equal chance. If it wasn't for music, I would have dropped out of school. It's not that I wasn't smart enough, I just wouldn't have had the motivation. It changed my life and made me who I am today. I'm very grateful for everything that my music teacher did for me and for the opportunities that I was given. The urban music program is vital, and for some students it's all they have.

Being a part of an urban music education program really made a huge impact on my life. I grew up in a strict household where freedom and independence were severely restricted. I wasn't allowed to make mistakes to teach myself right from wrong—I was told "this is right, that is wrong," no questions. Being in music allowed me to be free. I was able to express myself and make mistakes. My middle school teacher was the one who really pushed me to realize that it was ok to mess up. I remember crying in his office in middle school and him trying so hard to teach me that I wasn't perfect and that I was going to make mistakes—but that was okay and that was how I would learn. There and in high school, I was allowed to pick up an instrument and just try—no pressure to be perfect. I knew I could mess up and not get punished. Music was my freedom. Music also taught me things I couldn't learn from a book or classroom: tolerance, love, and acceptance. In our program, we were so diverse. We had Black, White, Asian, Latino, rich, poor, Catholic, Jewish students—everything. We went over to people's houses for dinners, families came to the performances, and you learned so much more about each other. Now, as an adult, I rarely feel uncomfortable. I feel like I can fit in anywhere I go because I have been exposed to so many different people.

I started playing an instrument in fifth grade but didn't really start to get serious until seventh grade. Up until that point, I had been going down "the wrong path," if you will. I had been hanging out with kids that were getting into trouble, serious trouble. It started innocent, stealing a candy bar from the corner store or some other petty shoplifting. It moved on to stealing Philly Blunts or some other type of smokes when nobody could snatch some from their parents. We had older friends (brothers or cousins of somebody we knew) that were getting into gang-banging. They encouraged us to help them break into houses and steal cars. Some of my friends were in juvenile before we even reached middle school. Some changed and some didn't.

Some started committing armed robbery and serving harder time. That was the path I was headed down. However, my middle school band teacher had some kind of way about him. There was some kind of love that he had for his students. It's odd to think about really. The love was similar to that of a parent. I'm blessed to have parents that truly love me and wish the best success for me. When you're a teen you don't see that. I was defiant toward my parents, as many teens are. I believe teachers hold some sort of strange teacher power. He had that parent-like love but because he wasn't my parent I didn't feel a compulsion to be defiant toward him. In fact, I felt like I couldn't let him down. I remember my first day of middle school. One of my good friends and his older brother were in the same school with me. My friend had been caught by the band teacher smoking at a building out back on the playground. My friend wasn't the kind of kid that took getting in trouble very well. He started to fight him and to make matters worse his older brother got into the fight as well. I don't know how he did it but somehow the band teacher got the younger brother in a headlock and walked him from the back of the playground to the school . . . all the while the older brother was jumping on his back, punching him and kicking him. The man was strong. I realized that he was the kind of teacher that didn't take any shit, nor was he the type of teacher to give a student undeserved shit. He had respect for us. It was that show of respect that changed me. The middle school years until the end of high school are so pivotal. I also believe that it was in part due to the nature of a music class. It's more laid back, more open, and not so institutional feeling. My music teacher showed that music allowed me an emotional outlet that I hadn't experienced before.

I've stopped playing my instrument and wish that I had never put it down. However, music still gives me that outlet. It's an outlet that my middle school teacher gave me and my high school teacher fine-tuned. Her teaching of music and the power behind the notes and the emotion that can come from a piece of music when played well . . . the fire she had about her when it came to music was inspirational, and it didn't stop with the music. I could tell that it carried through to the students. She cared about us, not only as students but as people. I have many friends in the teaching field (public schools, private schools, university) and they all say the same thing. There's a difference, a noticeable difference when a teacher teaches to students and when they're teaching to PEOPLE. The kids know when they're seen as people and they feel the respect that comes with that. Out of the four best teachers I've ever had in K-12, two of them are music teachers. There must be something to say for that.

REFERENCES

Abril, C. (2003). No hablo Ingles: Breaking the language barrier in music instruction. *Music Educators Journal, 89*(5), 38–43.

Abril, C. (2006). Teaching music in urban landscapes: Three perspectives. In C. Frierson-Campbell (Ed.), *Teaching music in the urban classroom* (Vol. 1, pp. 75–98). Lanham, MD: Rowman and Littlefield Education.

Ausmann, S. W. (1991). *Characteristics of inservice urban music teachers and preservice music teachers in Ohio and their attitudes toward teaching music in urban schools.* Unpublished doctoral dissertation, Ohio State University, Columbus.

Austin, J. (2013). *Into the black hole: Exploring motivation constructs and implications for music learning.* Presentation for the Annual University of Michigan Music Education Winter Lecture Series, Ann Arbor.

Barnett, J., & Hodson, D. (2001). Pedagogical context knowledge: Toward a fuller understanding of what good science teachers know. *Science Teacher Education, 85*, 426–453.

Bates, V. (2012). Social class and school music. *Music Educators Journal, 98*(33), 33–37. doi: 10.1177/0027432112442944

Bernstein, B. (1970). A critique of the concept of compensatory education. In D. Rubenstein & C. Stoneman (Eds.), *Education for democracy* (pp. 110–121). London: Penguin Books.

Bomer, R., Dworin, J. E., May, L., & Semingson, P. (2008). Miseducating teachers about the poor: A critical analysis of Ruby Payne's claims about poverty. *Teachers College Record, 110*(11), 2497–2531.

Bluestone, B., Stevenson, M., & Williams, R. (2008). *The urban experience: Economics, society, and public policy.* New York: Oxford.

Bobetsky, V. (2005). Exploring a community's heritage through a collaborative unit of study. *Music Educators Journal, 91*(5), 51–56.

Boyer-White, R. (1988). Reflecting cultural diversity in the music classroom. *Music Educators Journal, 75*(4), 50–54.

Bussey, J. (2007). *Math teaching that counts: Successful teachers of urban, African American middle school students.* Unpublished doctoral dissertation, Wayne State University, Detroit, MI.

Chen, K., Sheth, A., Krejci, J., & Wallace, J. (2003, August). *Understanding differences in alcohol use among high school students in two different communities.* Paper presented at the annual meeting of the American Sociological Association, Atlanta, GA.

Chen, A., Darst, P. W., & Pangrazi, R. P. (2001). An examination of situational interest and its sources. *British Journal of Educational Psychology, 71*, 383–400.

Clandinin, D. J. (1989). Developing rhythm in teaching: The narrative study of a beginning teacher's personal practical knowledge of classrooms. *Curriculum Inquiry, 19*(2), 121–141.

Compton-Lilly, C. (2003). *Reading families: The literate lives of urban children.* New York: Teachers College Press.

Cross, W. E. (1971). The Negro to Black conversion experience. *Black World, 20*(9), 13–27.

Csikszentmihalyi, M. (1990). *Flow: The psychology of optimal experience.* New York: Harper & Row.

Darling-Hammond, L., & Sclan, E. (1996). Who teaches and why: Building a profession for 21st century schools. In J. Sikula, T. Buttery, & E. Guyton (Eds.), *The handbook of research on teacher education* (pp. 67–101). New York: Macmillan.

Delpit, L. (1995). *Other people's children: Cultural conflict in the classroom.* New York: New Press.

Diala, C. C., Muntaner, C., & Walrath, C. (2004). Gender, occupational, and socioeconomic correlates of alcohol and drug abuse among U.S. rural, metropolitan, and urban residents. *American Journal of Drug and Alcohol Abuse, 30*(2), 409–428.

Eccles, J., Adler T. F., Futterman R., Goff, S. B., Kaczala C. M., et al. 1983. Expectancies, values, and academic behaviors. In J. T. Spence (Ed.), *Achievement and achievement motivation*, pp. 75–146. San Francisco: Freeman.

Economic Policy Institute. (2002). *The state of working class America 2002–03.* Washington, DC: Author.

Edgar, S. (2012). *Approaches of high school facilitative instrumental music educators in response to the social and emotional challenges of students.* Unpublished doctoral dissertation, University of Michigan, Ann Arbor.

Ensign, J. (2003). Including culturally relevant math in an urban school. *Educational Studies, 34*, 414–23.

Feick, D. L., & Rhodewalt, F. (1997). The double-edged sword of self-handicapping: Discounting, augmentation, and the protection and enhancement of self-esteem. *Motivation and Emotion, 21*(2), 145–161.

Fitzpatrick, K. (2008). *A mixed methods portrait of urban instrumental music teaching.* Unpublished doctoral dissertation, Northwestern University, Evanston, IL.

Fitzpatrick, K. (2012). Cultural diversity and the formation of identity: Our role as music teachers. *Music Educators Journal, 98*(53).

Fitzpatrick, K., Henninger, J., & Taylor, D. (2014). Access and retention of marginalized populations within undergraduate music education programs. *Journal of Research in Music Education, 62*(2), 105–127.

Flagg, M. (2006). Five simple steps to becoming a music teacher leader in an urban school. In C. Frierson-Campbell (Ed.), *Teaching music in the urban classroom* (Vol. 2, pp. 35–46). Lanham, MD: Rowman and Littlefield Education.

Galea, S., Ahern, J., Tracy, M., & Vlahov, D. (2007). Neighborhood income and income distribution and the use of cigarettes, alcohol, and marijuana. *American Journal of Preventive Medicine, 32*(6), 195–202.

Goetze, Mary. (2000). Challenges of performing diverse cultural music. *Music Educators Journal, 87*(1), 23–25, 48.

Gorski, P. (2008). The myth of the culture of poverty. *Poverty and Learning, 65*(7), 32–36.

Grossman, P. (1990). *The making of a teacher: Teacher knowledge and teacher education.* New York: Teachers College Press.

Haberman, M. (1993). Predicting the success of urban teachers (the Milwaukee Trials). *Action in Teacher Education, 15*(3), 1–5.

Haberman, M. (2005). *Star teachers of children in poverty.* Indianapolis, IN: Kappa Delta Pi Publications.

Haberman, M., & Post, L. (1992). Does direct experience change education students' perceptions of low-income minority children? *Midwestern Educational Researcher, 5*(2), 29–31.

Haberman, M., & Post, L. (1998). Teachers for multicultural schools: The power of selection. *Theory into Practice, 37*(2), 96.

Haycock, K. (1998). No more settling for less. *Thinking, 4*(1), 3–12.

Hayes, D. (1993). Educating the hip-hop generation: Communication barriers offset efforts to reach young minds. *Black Issues in Higher Education, 10*(14), 30–33.

Heilig, J. V., Cole, H., & Aguilar, A. (2010). From Dewey to No Child Left Behind: The evolution and devolution of public arts education. *Arts Education Policy Review, 111,* 136–145.

Isaac-Johnson, D. (2007). *Creating culturally relevant technological operas in an urban school.* Unpublished doctoral dissertation, University of Missouri–Columbia.

Irvine, J. J. (2010). *Foreword.* In H. R. Milner (Ed.), *Culture, curriculum, and identity in education.* New York: Palgrave Macmillan.

Iversen, R. R., & Farber, N. (1996). Transmission of family values, work, and welfare among poor urban black women. *Work and Occupations, 23*(4), 437–460.

Jorgensen, E. (2003). Western Classical music and general education. *Philosophy of Music Education Review, 11*(2), 130–140.

Kennedy White, K. (2006). *Exploring relationships between lived experiences of teachers who are culturally competent and their success with diverse students.* Unpublished doctoral dissertation, University of Colorado at Denver.

Kolditz, T. A., & Arkin, R. M. (1982). An impression management interpretation of the self-handicapping strategy. *Journal of Personality and Social Psychology, 43,* 492–502.

Kozol, J. (1991). *Savage inequalities: Children in America's schools.* Crown: New York.

Krieger, N., Williams, D. R., & Moss, N. E. (1997). Measuring social class in US public health research: Concepts, methodologies, and guidelines. *Annual Review of Public Health, 18*(34), 341–378.

Kutz, E., & Roskelly, H. (1991). *An unquiet pedagogy: Transforming practice in the English classroom.* Portsmouth, NH: Heinemann.

Ladson-Billings, G. (1994). *The dreamkeepers: Successful teachers of African American children.* San Francisco, CA: Jossey-Bass.

Lareau, A., & Horvat, E. (1999). Moments of social inclusion and exclusion: Race, class, and cultural capital in family-school relationships. *Sociology of Education, 72,* 37–53.

Lareau, A. (2011). *Unequal childhoods: Class, race, and family life.* Berkeley: University of California Press.

Lee, V., & Burkham, D. (2002). *Inequality at the starting gate: Social background differences in achievement as children begin school.* Washington, DC: Economic Policy Institute.

Leichter, H. J. (Ed.). (1978). *Families and communities as educators.* New York: Teachers College Press.

Marsh, H. W. (1984). Relations among dimensions of self-attribution, dimensions of self-concept, and academic achievements. *Journal of Educational Psychology, 76*(6), 1291–1308.

Marshall, H. (2006). Restructuring and partnering in urban schools: Change, cooperation, and courage. In C. Frierson-Campbell (Ed.), *Teaching music in the urban classroom* (Vol. 2, pp. 161–178). Lanham, MD: Rowman and Littlefield Education.

Milner, H. R. (2010). *Start where you are, but don't stay there: Understanding diversity, opportunity gaps, and teaching in today's classrooms.* Cambridge, MA: Harvard Education Press.

Milner, H. R. (2012). But what is urban education? *Urban Education, 47,* 556–561. doi: 10.1177/0042085912447516

Mixon, K. (2005). Building your instrumental music program in an urban school. *Music Educators Journal, 91*(3),15–23.

Morrell, E., & Duncan-Andrade, J. (2002). Promoting academic literacy with urban youth through engaging hip-hop culture. *English Journal, 91*(6), 88–92.

Negy, C., Shreve, T., Benson, B., & Uddin, N. (2004). Ethnic identity, self-esteem, and ethnocentrism: A study of social identity versus multicultural theory of development. *Cultural Diversity and Ethnic Minority Psychology, 9*(4), 333–334.

Nieto, S. (2000). *Affirming diversity: The sociopolitical context of multicultural education* (3rd ed.). Boston: Pearson.

Ohio Department of Education. (2005). *Enrollment by student demographic (Northland High School)* [Data file]. Retrieved from http://bireports.education.ohio.gov/PublicDW/asp/Main.aspx

Orfield, G., Losen, D., Wald, J., & Swanson, C. (2004). *Losing our future: How minority youth are being left behind by the graduation rate crisis.* Cambridge, MA: Civil Rights Project at Harvard University.

Robinson, N. (2004). Who is "at-risk" in the music classroom? *Music Educators Journal, 90*(4), 38–43.

Robinson, K. (2006). White teacher, students of color: Culturally responsive pedagogy for elementary general music in communities of color. In Carol Frierson-Campbell (Ed.), *Teaching Music in the Urban Classroom* (Vol. 1, pp. 35–56). Lanham, MD: Rowman and Littlefield Education.

Saxe, L., Kadushin, C., Tighe, E., Rindskopf, D., & Beveridge, A. (2001). *National evaluation of the fighting back program: General population surveys, 1995–1999.* New York: City University of New York Graduate Center.

Smith, C. (1997). Access to string instruction in American public schools. *Journal of Research in Music Education, 45*(4), 650–662.

Smith, J. (2006). The challenges of urban teaching: Young urban music educators at work. In C. Frierson-Campbell (Ed.), *Teaching music in the urban classroom* (Vol. 1, pp. 57–74). Lanham, MD: Rowman and Littlefield Education.

Tatum, B. (2004). Family life and school experience: Factors in the racial identiy development of Black youth in White communities. *Journal of Social Issues, 60*(1), 117–135.

Tatum, B. (2007). *Can we talk about race? And other conversations in an era of school resegregation.* Boston: Beacon Press.

Ungemah, L. (2014). "Student teachers": What I learned from students in a high-poverty urban high school. In P. Gorski and J. Landsman (Eds.), *The poverty and education reader.* Sterling, VA: Stylus Publishing.

Wallick, M. D. (1998). A comparison study of the Ohio Proficiency Test results between fourth-grade string pullout students and those of matched ability. *Journal of Research in Music Education, 46*(2), 239–247.

Washington, E. D. (1989). A componential theory of culture and its implications for African-American identity. *Equity and Excellence, 24*(2), 24–30.

Welner, K., & Carter, P. (2013). Achievement gaps arise from opportunity gaps. In P. Carter and K. Welner, *Closing the Opportunity Gap* (pp. 1–11). New York: Oxford.

Wilson, W. J. (1997). *When work disappears*. New York: Random House.

Zhao, Y. (2007). *A case study of the impact of urban immersion teacher preparation and urban school workplace on the perceived self-efficacy, persistence and institutional commitment of urban school teachers*. Unpublished doctoral dissertation, University of Massachusetts, Amherst.

INDEX